THE MUSICIAN IN UNIT G

Mockingbird Place

LEE SWIFT

Created with Vellum

Acknowledgments

This one is for all the innocent men and women who have been imprisoned wrongfully.

Mockingbird Place

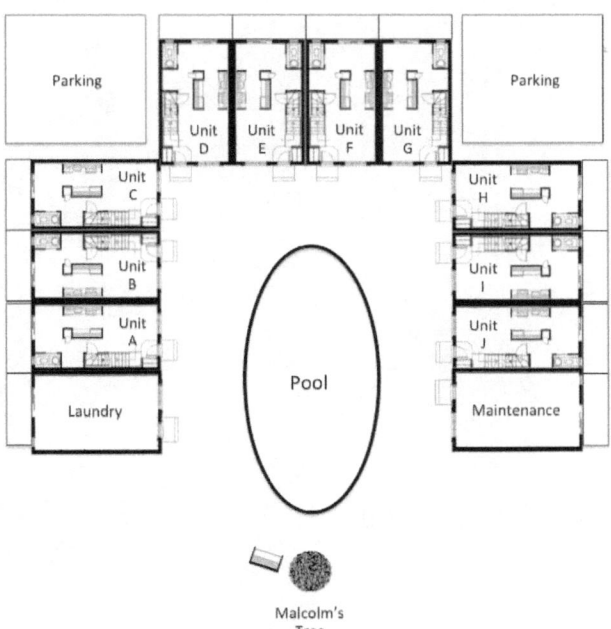

Parking

Parking

Unit D

Unit E

Unit F

Unit G

Unit C

Unit H

Unit B

Unit I

Unit A

Unit J

Laundry

Pool

Maintenance

Malcolm's Tree

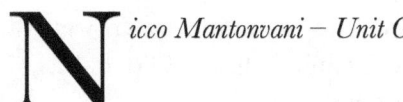

Chapter 1

Nicco Mantonvani – Unit G

AS I WALK OUT of the back of Unit F with the last load of my stuff, I notice a black Ford Mustang parked in one of the visitor's spots. I've seen it a couple of times. I wonder who it belongs to and who they're visiting. Damn, it's a hot car. In my old neighborhood, all the kids were crazy about Mustangs and swore we would all own one. Most of us wanted black, just like that one.

I still wouldn't mind having one.

When I try Unit G's patio gate, it doesn't budge. Josh must have locked it.

I go around the building to the front so I can use the key he gave me.

A man in a suit is knocking on my new apartment's door.

How the hell did he get in through the gates?

Sarah and Martha, who we lovingly call "S & M", along with Oliver are the owners of Mockingbird Place. The trio had the entire complex fenced and gated after the arson of Eli's apartment several months ago. To get onto the property now, a person must have the code to the keypad.

I look at the stranger. "You need something, mister?"

The man turns to me. "I'm looking for Josh White. Do you know where he is?"

"Who's asking? And can you tell me how you got through our security gates?"

He narrows his eyes and stares at me in a way I don't like at all. "Just tell Josh I was looking for him."

"Who the hell is looking for him?"

"He'll know." The man looks at the things I'm carrying. "Moving day?"

I ignore his question and push past him to Josh's and my door, bringing out my key.

His face darkens. "You live with Josh?"

"Oh, so now you have questions you want me to answer." I know I'm coming across hard, but I can't help it. Old habits, I suppose, or maybe I just don't like this guy.

"Good point. The answer to your question is Grayson. I'm Mr. Grayson. And the answer to my question about you living here with Josh?"

"I'll let him know you stopped by." I shut the door on the prick.

When Josh gets back from his band practice with Chad and Franki, I'm going to find out who the hell Mr. Grayson really is. There's something about him that just doesn't mesh with me. He doesn't seem like the kind of guy Josh would be friends with, and definitely not someone he would date. Did Josh give him the code to get in? I have more questions but they'll have to wait until Josh gets here.

I look around my new apartment. It's quite different in décor than either of the other two places I've lived in at the complex. Josh has a brown leather sofa with several folding chairs stacked against the wall in the living area and a table and chairs near the kitchen. The rest of the downstairs space is all about music. It looks more like a studio than an apartment. There are microphones, amplifiers, and a variety of musical instruments, including a sick set of drums. Instead of typical paintings you would find in most apartments, in Unit G there are guitars hanging on the walls, as well as posters from gigs where the band has played.

Some might find the space a little less inviting, or at the very least a place difficult to entertain. But for me, I like the energy. Music is Josh's life. I love his band, Red Shimmer, which is made up of him, Chad, and Franki. They are amazing. And now that I will be living here, I'll have a front row seat to their practices. Win-win.

Moving never takes long since I have so little, but I really hope this is the last time. Since getting out of prison, this is the third unit at Mockingbird Place I've lived in.

The first one was from my prison cell to my younger brother Tony's apartment, Unit J. Then he fell in love with Stephen, an Episcopalian priest and a man with a big heart. Most of us at the complex have been attending the Episcopal Church of the Beloved Disciple to support Stephen. It's a warm and welcoming place. No judgment. Stephen's biggest fan there is Mrs. Clark, a ninety-year-old lady, who has been a member since she was a teenager. Mrs. Clark has adopted Tony, Stephen, and I as her own. We're all crazy about her and her weekly cookie deliveries.

As Stephen and Tony's relationship became permanent, I knew I needed to give them some space. So for the second move I took over Stephen's apartment, Unit F. He's the one who helped exonerate my record. I owe him so much, but mostly I'm thrilled that he treats Tony so well.

Blake became my roommate for only a month because he and Chad had a holiday fling. And to no one's surprise, that turned into something permanent too.

That's the reason for the third move, this move. I'm going to be living with Josh. I don't make enough at the airplane charter company to live on my own yet. Until I get my pilot's license, I have to have a roommate. Besides, Josh has everything that a home needs that I don't. I only have one plate, one set of silverware, a towel, a set of sheets, my bed, some clothes, and not much else.

The added benefit is my new roommate is sexy as hell. So far, I

haven't picked up on any signals from Josh that he might be interested in me more than just helping with the rent. Why would he? I
haven't been out of prison that long. Besides, Josh's rep as a player
would not fit into what I want in my life. It may seem crazy for me
to want what Tony and Stephen have, but I do want that. I want a
family. I want kids. I want the white picket fence with the minivan
parked in the driveway. That dream is what kept me alive in prison.
I'm not letting it go now. Or ever. I'm not sure where or if Josh fits
into my dream. I guess time will tell.

Time? That's something very different in the big house than out
here in the real world. I remember lying on my hard prison bed
staring at the concrete ceiling, counting the seconds one by one as
they ticked by. It was like trying to walk through tar but getting
nowhere. To pass the time I memorized every detail of my six by
eight foot steel-walled home. The bars were six across and twenty
vertical. There were five gouges in the floor and seventy-three
scratches on the wall.

"Stop it, Nicco. You're not there. You're here. You're out."

I'm still not used to my freedom. Days fly by so fast. And I can
go anywhere, anytime, whenever I want. It's kind of weird after so
long on the inside, where my every move was monitored, my every
second controlled. I remember Old Joe, who was a prison mate of
mine, telling me how hard it would be to acclimate when I got out. I
didn't understand. Now I do.

Spending time with Tony and his wonderful friends and neighbors at Mockingbird Place has made it easier for me to adjust. I still
have a lot to work through, but I'm making great strides every day.
Everyone around here shows me what it really means to enjoy life. I
won't waste a second on trivial matters or dead ends. The past is the
past.

I walk upstairs, which is quite the contrast to downstairs, with
my last load. On this floor are two bedrooms and a bath. I love my
room. It has a view of the pool and a huge closet, not that I need
one that big with so few clothes. Josh offered to help me repaint the
walls, since they are purple, a remnant of Chad's taste. I declined
Josh's offer. I really like the color, a complete contrast to the gray

palate I had to endure the past ten years. The brighter the better. The space is very sparse since I only have a bed, but it still makes me smile. Fifteen by fifteen feet. It's massive and I love it.

As I put the last of my things away, I hear Josh come in downstairs through the back door.

"Hey, Nicco. You here?"

"Yes, upstairs in my room. I'll be right down."

"Awesome. I brought some Chinese for us."

I close the closet door. "Sounds great, Josh."

I hurry downstairs to find him opening a bottle of wine. Josh is a very good-looking guy, dark blond hair, sometimes clean-shaven, sometimes close trimmed, blue eyes, and a smile that melts a person's heart.

"I didn't realize I was hungry until you mentioned Chinese." I pick up one of the little white boxes and open it. "Ah. Sesame chicken. Love it. How much do I owe you?"

"My treat." He fills our wine glasses. "Consider this meal a welcoming gift, and I really mean that, Nicco. I've been lonely since Chad moved in with Blake. I'm glad to have you living here with me."

"I'm glad too. I get that you've been lonely. You and Chad are close, being in the band and all." I sit down and take a sip of the wine. "This is good."

"Malbec. My favorite." Josh sits down and also sips on his wine.

I take several bites of the food. "Delicious. Thanks again for this."

"You're welcome. It is good, isn't it?"

"Sure is. Where is it from?"

"A new place. Mr. Wong's Wok. It was across the street from our gig last week in Deep Ellum. I thought I'd give it a try."

"Glad you did. I love it." I sample the crab puffs, which are amazing. "I feel like I've died and gone to heaven."

He smiles. "This is the best Chinese food I've ever eaten. We'll have to tell Chad and Franki about the place. They love Chinese food more than anyone I know."

"I've heard. By the way, I want to thank you and them for

helping my mom land that job at the studio. As I'm sure you're aware, she needed that break."

"No big deal. And from what I saw at our last recording session, she's doing a great job. Everyone loves her."

"I'm glad. Seems like you guys are really catching some big breaks for your band lately."

"We sure have." Josh sighs, which surprises me. "I never thought Red Shimmer would get so much press."

"Isn't that a good thing for the band? Press?"

"Oh, yeah. Sure. Just a lot to take in so suddenly."

Seeing the look on his face, I realize there's more to it than he's admitting. What other secrets does Josh have, or am I just imagining things? Suspicion helped me survive for a long time, but maybe I need to be more trusting. "Hey, I forgot to mention that a Mr. Grayson came by and was asking about you. Don't know how you know him, but he was quite nosy and asking a lot of questions."

Josh puts down his glass. "What did you say to him?"

I know how to read people, and what I'm reading off of Josh troubles me. There's something odd about how he feels about this Grayson dude. "I told him you weren't here."

"Anything else?"

"No, but I was carrying the last box of my stuff inside. He figured out I was moving in with you."

"Damn it."

I can see a storm brewing in his blue eyes. "Josh, something wrong?"

"No. It's fine. I just should have told Grayson about you already."

"It may be none of my business, but who is he?"

"Uh…no one important." He stands. "I'll clean this up later."

Nope. I'm not imagining things. Something is definitely off between Josh and Grayson. "I'll take care of it. You bought, so I'll take care of the mess."

"Thanks." He rushes upstairs.

I hear him shut his bedroom door. I'm no Sherlock Holmes, but it's very obvious that he's calling this Grayson dude right now.

As I clear the table, I wonder what kind of hold this creep has over Josh.

When I walk upstairs, Josh's door is still closed. As expected, I can hear him talking on the phone.

"Yes, he's my fucking roommate and it's none of your business." Josh's volume continues to rise.

I'm no eavesdropper, but I can't help but hear. And if he's in trouble, I'm not going to sit on the sidelines.

"Fine. Do whatever the hell you have to do. I'm not an idiot, Grayson. I will meet you at the regular time and place, as always. Don't worry about that. Now leave me alone."

I step into my bedroom and stare at his closed door. It's obvious that Josh is in over his head about something. About what? I don't know yet, but I'm going to find out.

Chapter 2

J*osh*

"JOSH, I can't and won't leave you alone." Grayson's voice comes through my phone loud and clear, as usual. "You know that."

"And you know how much I've given up, Grayson." I sit down on my bed, exhausted not just from this call, but also from everything that has happened to me since that awful night in Chicago. "I want a normal life, just like everyone else."

"You're not like everyone else. Not anymore."

"I know I'm not, and I'm sick of it. I'm sick of this life and I'm sick of you."

"I'm sorry you feel that way, but you know you should have told me about this new roommate of yours."

"Why should I? I already know he's a good guy." I'm not about to tell Grayson that Nicco served prison time. Let him find out for himself. It won't change how I feel. I want Nicco as my roommate.

That's final. Besides, Nicco's record was exonerated. He was innocent, but I know that won't change how Grayson will see him. Grayson's a guilty-until-proven-innocent kind of guy, not the other way around.

Grayson sighed. "Don't be stupid. You know why you should have told me."

"Yeah, I know why. So you could continue ruling my life."

"It's for your own good. You're taking too many risks. You should have quit that band when I told you to a long time ago. Now, your face is plastered on local TV and newspapers. Someone might put two and two together, Josh."

"It's been over five years. Besides, it's local, not national." Despite my insistent tone, I know he's right.

Things are getting way too hot around here for me, and I will not take chances that could get my friends hurt. Hell, I've already stayed longer than I should have. Chad and Franki are pushing to get us wider press. And with the title song on our CD "Wild and Wilder" hitting the top of local charts, I have no doubt that more press will be coming.

"Josh, are you still there?"

I'm going to have to do something soon, but I don't have to admit that to Grayson right now. "No one will figure out who I am."

"How can you be so sure?"

"Because, Grayson, no one knows my real name. Just like you. Your name isn't Grayson, so I guess that makes us both imposters."

"We can table the discussion about you staying in the band for now." Grayson doesn't normally let me win so easily. What's going on with him? "Before I hang up, I need to know your roommate's name."

"Find out for yourself." I click off the phone and toss it onto my bed.

This day definitely didn't turn out the way I wanted. I thought Nicco and I would have a nice first meal together with a couple of glasses of wine. Then, I had some ideas of how the rest of the time would go. I would kiss him. He would kiss me back.

I've made up my mind that I'm going to stop playing the role of manwhore. That's not me. Never has been. It's just an act that I've had to play to keep the guys I go out with from danger. But it's been seven years since the incident. How long do I have to keep looking over my shoulder? I want a chance at love and a real relationship.

I close my eyes, and an image of Nicco with his Italian god good looks fills my mind. Dark hair. Dark eyes. Full lips. Chiseled jaw line. A body that is rock solid. Impressive ink on both his muscled arms. And I've never met a more loyal guy in my life. What he did for his brother floors me. Tough and yet tender. I've seen how he acts with Oliver and Adam's infant twins and the other little kids around here. He's like a big overgrown Teddy bear. He's a man of few words, but when he speaks I'm amazed at his insight and intelligence, not to mention his quick wit. I still don't know how he can have such an upbeat attitude after spending all those years in prison for a crime he didn't commit.

Ever since Nicco moved to Mockingbird Place I haven't had a single night without dreaming about him. He's perfect for me. But who am I trying to kid? This is typical of my bad luck the last five years. Now that I found the possible man of my dreams, I have to leave.

I open my eyes and stare out of my window.

I will not take any chances that could endanger Nicco or Chad, Franki, or anyone else at Mockingbird Place. The truth is I'm going to be looking over my shoulder for the rest of my life. Why should I expect anyone else to? My friends have their own lives to live.

Realizing my fate will never change, frustration swirls inside me.

I curl my hands into fists.

How long before I have to disappear? A month? A week? I've stayed longer here than anywhere else. God, I'm going to miss this place so much. In the meantime, I've got to find someone to replace me in Red Shimmer. I also need to find Nicco a new roommate.

Damn it.

I take a deep breath. "We can't be together, but we can be room-mates. At least for now."

I walk out of my bedroom and head downstairs for a much-needed glass of wine. Nicco cleaned up our mess perfectly. There is no evidence that we had Chinese anywhere. Not a single crumb. He even found the stopper for the wine bottle. *Neat, too. He really is perfect.*

I get a fresh glass and fill it.

After a few sips, I grab an acoustic and begin strumming. Music is much better than wine when it comes to relieving my stress.

I look up and see Nicco coming down the stairs. "Sorry, I hope I didn't disturb you."

"Not at all. Keep playing. I love it."

"Cool. Pour yourself a glass of wine."

"I will." He points at the keyboard. "Mind if I join you?"

I'm shocked. "I didn't know you played. Of course you can join me."

"I hadn't played in years when I was sentenced. But I took it up again in prison. It was part of the rehabilitation efforts." After filling his glass, he sits down at the keyboard and smiles at me. "Don't judge. I'm not a pro like you."

"Hey, let's just have fun."

Nicco pounds out some chords and we're off.

I can't believe how great he plays and sings. We start with some classic rock, followed by pop, then jazz with a little soul thrown in.

Nicco twists on the stool and grabs a drumstick. "How about some EDM now?"

"Lead away, buddy."

To my utter shock, he's able to pound out a rhythm on my snare and keep playing the keyboard with his other hand.

When we finish, I turn to him. "Not a pro? Are you trying to hustle me? You're amazing. What other instruments do you play? Don't hold out on me, Nicco."

"I play a little guitar and a little bass."

"Just like you play a little piano and a little drums? Do you realize how talented you are?"

He shrugs. "The guys in Cell Block D liked when I played."

I laugh. "I bet they did."

"Seriously, music was the only way I stayed sane in prison. Even when I was a kid it was the best way for me to relieve my stress."

"I know exactly what you mean."

"I started taking piano lessons when Tony was born. Our father was still alive then and our life was so good." Nicco takes a sip of wine. "Sorry. I don't why I'm talking about my past so much."

"Don't be sorry." I reach over and touch his arm, thrilled that he's sharing with me. "It's the magic of music. Besides, I want to know about your past."

He looks at me with his dark, smoldering eyes.

Unable to look away for several shallow breaths, I realize I'm falling under his spell. "Uh...we should know more about each other, Nicco. We're roommates, after all."

He smiles. "Yes, we are."

"Tell me more about why you quit playing when you were a kid."

"Until my father passed away, life was beautiful. We had wonderful dinners every night. Mom loved to bake cookies back then. Whenever Dad got home from work, he would get on the floor and play games with Tony and me. But after he died our whole life changed. One day it was warm and sunny. The next day it was cold and dark. I just couldn't bring myself to play anymore."

"How old were you?"

"I was ten and Tony was four." He takes another sip of wine.

This is the most I've ever heard him say to anyone. I feel close to him and honored that he can be so honest with me.

"Let me open another bottle." I refill our glasses. "That must have been so difficult for you being so young."

"Yeah. It sucked, but someone had to take charge and try to fill the gap my dad left behind. My mother just couldn't do it. She fell totally apart and started drinking. Later, she began using after hooking up with a drug addict. I had to step up and take care of her and Tony. We were about to be evicted from our home. I needed money. So, I did the only thing I knew to do. I joined a gang and dirty cash started flowing my way. Right or wrong, I was able to pay all the bills and make sure there was food in the house for her and Tony."

"I can appreciate the moral dilemma you've had to suffer with. But if I was in your shoes and still a kid, I think I would have done the same thing. This may be a hard question, but didn't you resent your mother?"

He sighs. "Truthfully, yes, but I loved her so much. For years, I thought if I kept helping her she would snap out of it. She never did. So I had to stay, for my little brother." He looks down into his glass, clearly struggling with the past. "But I failed him, Josh."

"How can you say that?"

"Because I left him. Mom was high most of the time. I couldn't stand being around her. As soon as Tony turned twelve, I thought he would be okay living with her if I kept paying the bills, kept taking him to school, and kept buying the groceries. So I moved out." He closes his eyes tight. "And less than two months later I went to my mother's house and found her bastard boyfriend raping Tony. I should have stayed and protected him."

I put my arm around him. "Don't beat yourself up, Nicco. You're not to blame. The pervert was to blame, and now he's dead. I know the rest of your story, how your thug friends killed the bastard and then let you take the fall for the murder. How your own mother, in a drugged out haze, told the police you had killed her boyfriend. Nicco, you didn't deserve any of it. You lost ten years in prison for a crime you didn't commit. You're amazing. I wouldn't have been able to do it. And look at your brother Tony now. He's happy and in love. Sure, you made mistakes, but you are a big part of the reason he survived that nightmare."

He opens his eyes, which are brimming with tears. "He did survive, didn't he?"

"And so did you." I pull him in close, thinking about the boy he once was who had to face all that darkness alone. "I'll say it again, Nicco. You're fucking amazing."

He smiles and then leans in and kisses me lightly.

Even though I would love to make out with him all night, I know where that would lead—with my heart in jeopardy and his life in danger.

I fake a yawn. "We better get some sleep. I've got practice with the band tomorrow, and didn't you say that you have to be at the airport for work early?"

"I sure do. I have to rise and shine before the sun. Gage has me working the desk at seven. He's got four women he's flying to Las Vegas." Nicco stands and fixes his sexy eyes on me. "Thanks for the jam session, but most of all for this talk, Josh. You really have made me feel at home on day one. Next time, it'll be your turn to tell me about your past, okay?"

There's no way I can tell him anything about my life before. I can't even tell him my real name.

I smile, though my insides are storming with mixed emotions. "That's what roommates are for, Nicco. See you in the morning."

"In the morning. Goodnight, Josh." He sends me a wink and then heads up to his room.

Shit. What am I doing?

icco

I STRETCH out on my bed and stare at my new ceiling, shocked at how easy it was to open up to Josh. I've never talked to anyone about my past like I did with him. Prison taught me to keep most things to myself. It's a survival tool I still use. But tonight it was different with Josh. He treated me with respect and didn't look at me with eyes full of judgment, like I was still an ex-con.

I dreamed of my freedom for so long, but it's been difficult for me since I got out. I don't let it show, because no one needs to worry about me. I'm still learning how to survive on the outside. I took a chance giving Josh that kiss. Was it a mistake? It felt so natural, so right with him. Right now we're just roommates, but he didn't seem to mind the kiss. Who knows what might happen with us living together?

I smile, imagining all kinds of things I'd like to happen with Josh and me. But one thing I know for sure, I need to take it slow. He was so receptive when I told him about my past. But when I mentioned that the next time it would be his turn to tell me about his past, I saw a strange look come over him even though he voiced that it would be okay.

Why? Does it have something to do with that Grayson dude? It may be none of my business, but I'm going to get Josh to tell me what's going on between Grayson and him. There's something very fishy about Grayson. What if he is blackmailing Josh? Or worse? Whatever it is, I'll be there for him.

I glance at my clock. If I fall right to sleep, I'll get at least five hours before the alarm goes off. Not a chance of that happening. I've got too much on my mind, and besides, ten years in prison makes it hard for me to fall asleep. I always had to keep one eye open just to be safe. Old habits are hard to break, but I'm hopeful in time I'll get back to normal.

I close my eyes and start the ritual of counting sheep. "One. Two. Three." The image of white, fluffy, four-legged sheep jumping over a fence fills my mind. "Four. Five. Damn it. A black one again. Start over. One. Two…"

WHEN I HEAD to the bathroom to get ready for work, I'm shocked to see Josh's bedroom door open, his bed made, and no sign of him anywhere.

"Josh, you downstairs?"

No answer.

Where could he be at this hour? According to Chad, Josh was notorious for sleeping in when they lived together. I thought he hated mornings.

After a quick shower and getting dressed, I walk downstairs and find a note next to the coffeepot.

Nicco,

Coffee is ready to go. Just hit the start button. I have an early meeting that I forgot about. See you at home tonight.

Josh

A meeting before seven in the morning? That doesn't make any sense. Is he with Grayson? That's the only thing I can come up with. I really would like to call Josh to find out, but of course I can't. Instead, I'm going to be thinking about it all day and wondering what is going on with him. Is he in real trouble?

I WALK into the office of McBain Charters and Pilot School. Gage McBain, one of the three siblings who owns the company, is sitting behind the counter. Liza, his sister, who works with me booking the charters, is getting the coffee made.

Gage looks up at me. "Hey, sexy."

"You talking to me?" I tease back.

Liza grins. "Who else would he be talking to?"

"Some sexy guy, I guess."

"Quit underestimating yourself, Nicco. You know you're hot as hell." Gage has been flirting with me since I interviewed for the job.

It's harmless fun. Gage flirts with every guy who walks in here. Though quite good-looking, he's not my type. Gage is a total manwhore.

So why am I so attracted to Josh? He and Gage have the same reputation. Everyone knows Josh kicks his dates to the curb after two or three nights. He's a manwhore, too, but there's something about what happened last night that tells me he just hasn't met the right guy.

"Nicco? You still with us?" Gage asks, bringing me back to the here and now.

"Yeah. Just need some coffee." I walk over the coffeepot.

Liza fills a cup and hands it to me. "I have a message from your brother, Tony. He and his husband are dropping by around noon to take you to lunch."

"Thanks." I come around the counter and sit down in front of the computer. "Gage, what time are your passengers arriving?"

"Any minute now. Liza, handle the desk for a little bit. I want

Nicco to do the preflight checklist with me." He turns to me. "It'll be good practice for you."

I grab the clipboard and follow him to the door. Working here has been great. Gage and his brother Doug have been helping me get my pilot's license. Jaris gave me my medical. I've already passed the written and have been up with Gage and Doug many times. I still haven't had my solo flight yet, but I feel I'm ready for it. My goal is to get my commercial license and work here at McBain. Something about being up in the sky gives me such a feeling of real freedom and exhilaration.

Gage watches me go through the entire checklist. "Great job. You didn't forget a thing."

"Thanks." I hand the clipboard over to him. "You and your brother are good instructors."

"I appreciate the compliment. Let's go to dinner tonight when I get back from Vegas. I have some things I want to talk to you about."

Is this about work, my flying lessons, or something else? I'm not sure, but there's only one way to find out. "Sounds good. What time?"

"I'll pick you up at seven. You like steak?"

"I do." Needing to stay in control of the situation, I add, "Tell me where and I'll meet you there."

He nods and writes down the address. "Looking forward to it, Nicco."

I need to say something to make sure he isn't thinking of this dinner as a date. But before I get a chance to open my mouth, Liza walks out with the charter passengers.

She smiles and motions to the plane. "Here we are, ladies. Nicco, can you grab some waters for them?"

"My pleasure." As I walk away, I hear the ladies giggling and stating they think I'm hot. Hopefully, Josh thinks so.

I walk back to the office, knowing I'll just have to find out the hard way what's on Gage's mind tonight. Worst case, I'll get to make it clear to him at dinner that there is no chance for us to be more than just coworkers and friends.

After Gage takes off with our charter customers, Liza and I get back to work.

At noon, as expected, Tony and Stephen enter the office. What I didn't expect was they brought my mother with them.

She's like her old self again. Beautiful. Warm. Full of hope. And most of all, confident in herself. Quite the contrast from when she was using. Seeing her this way reminds me of how it was when Dad was still alive. Still, there are old scars and doubt we have to overcome. Tony is suspicious that she might relapse. I'm concerned too, but hopeful. She really is working with her sponsor and has made incredible strides in her recovery.

"Hi, guys." I give Mom a hug. "You're a nice surprise. I didn't know you were coming."

"I never turn down a chance to see my two handsome boys." She kisses me on the cheek. "This morning, Tony and Stephen came over to give me some tips on using Word and Excel. They invited me to join you. I hope you don't mind."

"I'm thrilled." I turn to Liza. "I'll be back in an hour."

"No rush. Take your time and enjoy your family. It's a slow day."

"Thanks."

We walk out the door to Stephen's car.

"Look, Nicco," Tony says, motioning to a car at the far end of the parking lot. "I remember you loved black Mustangs."

How strange. "Still do. Seems like I'm seeing them everywhere lately. Where are we going to lunch?"

"I suggested this little diner on Cedar Springs to your brother and Stephen," Mom says. "I've been once with my boss and coworkers."

Stephen drives out of the airport. "I've heard the food and service is great, and the prices are very reasonable."

"Sounds good to me." I turn to Mom. "How's the new job going?"

"After getting the lesson from Tony and Stephen, I feel so much better now. I'm sure my new boss will be impressed too."

"From what I've heard from Josh, Chad, and Franki, you're making quite the impression with everyone."

"I love it. The people I work with are great and Mr. Paulson has been very gracious and understanding. He even took me to lunch the other day to welcome me to the team."

"Oh, really?" Tony, who is in the front next to Stephen, turns and looks at her. "Seems to me that an office romance might be brewing."

"Oh, stop. You're being silly."

Is he? I feel my gut tighten. Does Mr. Paulson have romantic ideas for my mother? After my father died, my mom hasn't had good luck with men. In my opinion, the last thing she needs to do is to get entangled with someone.

Mom continues telling us about her new job. "I was so nervous when I first started, but I'm getting the hang of it now. I have to thank your friends for getting me the gig."

"Gig?" Tony smiles. "You really are fitting in with the entertainment circles."

"I have to. Some of the biggest names in music come through Mr. Paulson's recording studio. I know I'm just the receptionist right now, but I have bigger dreams to learn more. Mr. Paulson noticed how interested I was and he told me that he wants to teach me the ins and outs of the business. He really is just as terrific as your friends said he was. I would like to make dinner for their whole band. It's the least I can do. Would you mind asking Josh when would be a good time?"

"Sure." I remember what a great cook she was when I was a kid. "I'm sure they would appreciate one of your home cooked meals."

After we get seated at the restaurant, Stephen gets a call. "It's the church. Excuse me. I'll be right back."

He walks outside to take the call.

"That man of mine loves his work, but he's way too busy." Tony stares at Stephen, who we can see through the diner's big glass window. "The church needs to get him some help. It's grown so much. The membership has doubled since he became the rector. I wish there was something I could do."

"Why can't *you* do something?" I ask him.

"What do you mean? Me? What could I do? I'm just an MMA fighter."

Mom shakes her head. "Just an MMA fighter? You are so much more than that. Look at me. Without your help and advice, I wouldn't be where I am today."

"But you're my mother. That's what I'm supposed to do and what I want to do."

"And Stephen is your husband," I tell him. "You've admitted he needs help. Step up and help him."

"I'm not sure I'm qualified, but I have been thinking about hanging up the boxing gloves."

Clearly shaken, Stephen walks back to our table. "I'm so sorry but I have to go. One of our members had a stroke and is at the hospital."

"Who is it?" Tony asks, his eyes full of concern.

"Mrs. Clark," he chokes out.

"Oh, no."

He leans down and hands Tony his keys. "I already have Uber on the way. Enjoy lunch with your mom and brother."

Tony stands and hands me the keys. "I'm going with him, if you don't mind."

"I completely understand." I close my eyes.

How often has that sweet lady knocked on my door with a plate of cookies? I remember the first night that Tony, Stephen, and I took her to dinner and I told her about my time in prison. She smiled and reminded me that St. Paul, who was also innocent, lived many years in prison too. "But even the prisoners who are guilty, God forgives. Who am I to judge?" I knew then that she didn't think less of me or anyone else.

I open my eyes. "Mom, why don't we go with them? Stephen could cancel his Uber. We can grab lunch at the hospital. I can Uber back to the airport afterward."

Mom nods. "Let's go, boys."

Chapter 4

J *osh*

SITTING in the nondescript beige office, I lean across Grayson's desk. "I can't keep up with this charade. I can't keep lying to these people. I care about them. The lies have to stop. Things have to change."

Grayson brings out an unlit cigar and puts it between his lips. He hasn't smoked in over a year, but this little habit of his has continued. I've noticed it always gives him a pause so that he can obviously have an extra moment to think.

The pause also gives me a few precious seconds to clear my own head.

As I lean back in the chair, I remember the note I left Nicco hours ago. It was all lies. There was no early morning meeting. I always meet with Grayson after lunch. It's what we've done since this whole thing started. I just couldn't face Nicco. Not after how close I felt to him last night. My guard was down. Another glance from him and I would have spilled every brutal detail. That wouldn't have been smart. Selfish? Yes. But not smart. I just needed a moment. Too bad I didn't have Grayson's cigar to chew on.

But what did the extra time get me? Not a damn thing. I drove around for hours and hours, trying to figure out what I could do to make things better with Nicco. I didn't come up with any answers. My situation seems impossible. Is there an answer? A solution? A way out? I just don't know. I feel trapped in limbo. *Or is it hell?*

Grayson removes the cigar from his lips. "What do you want to do, Josh? Get yourself killed?"

"Of course I don't want to get myself killed. Why do you think I've been playing this game with you? But it's been five years. The people at Mockingbird Place are my family now. I don't want to lose them too." *Definitely hell.* "I wish I'd never testified against Thompson."

"Don't say that." His face reddens. One thing I've learned about Grayson, the man is passionate about justice. "You put that murdering bastard away. No telling how many lives you've saved."

"Really? The only thing that happened was another *murdering bastard* took his place and started running his business. Nothing changed, Grayson."

"That's not true. Yes, Clyde Walker is running Chicago's South-side mob's criminal enterprises now, but he doesn't hold a candle to the power or cruelty Theodore 'Teddy' Thompson had. No one in the organization seems to respect him, and that is in our favor."

"Your favor, not mine. I don't give a damn anymore. Besides, Thompson is going before the parole board next week. Everything I did to put him away might go up in smoke. How in the hell did he get a hearing after only serving seven years of his sentence?"

"Expensive syndicate lawyers. His allies can't stand Walker and are hoping to find a loophole to get Thompson's freedom and put him back in the power seat. But there's no way Thompson will get out. I spoke to the DA this morning. This hearing is just a formality."

"Formality? I don't get it. None of it. He killed that man in cold blood. He deserves to rot in prison, not to have a parole hearing."

"True. Hopefully he'll spend the rest of his miserable life behind bars."

"Hopefully? See. Even you aren't sure how long he'll serve." I clutch the arms of the chair. "The price I've had to pay for being in the wrong place at the wrong time and seeing something I shouldn't have has been far too high. I was just an innocent bystander who only wanted a career in music. That's all. And now, finally, after all this time, I have a real chance to reach my dream with my friends."

"Use your head, Josh. I'm not trying to be cruel, just honest. This is how it is, like it or not. It's reality."

"It's *my* reality. It feels like an eternity since your team whisked me away from Thompson's murder trial and gave me my first new identity."

"Michael Long. Miami. I remember."

"That lasted only three months before the situation was compromised. And then I was Kevin Curtis in Oregon for just four months."

"Yes. I know the entire list of your seven last identities, but you've been in Dallas as Josh White for over five years now. I'd call that a success, wouldn't you?"

"No, I wouldn't call that a success. That's not what you promised me when this started. You promised me a brand new life, and no one else would get hurt. I want six more months here, Grayson."

"Impossible. Being in that band has exposed you, not to mention the issue of your new roommate, Niccolo Mantonvani." He chews on his cigar, before continuing. "The ex-con."

"He's not an ex-con. Nicco was exonerated."

Grayson opens the drawer and pulls out a thick folder. "Yes, he was, but that doesn't change the rest of his record. I've only had a chance to give his file a cursory review, but it's clear that Mantonvani has been in and out of trouble since he was twelve years old."

"I know that, but you have no idea what kind of childhood he had to endure."

Grayson shakes his head. "Every criminal has a sad story to tell.

Trust me. Prisons are filled with people who claim they are innocent victims."

"Again, Grayson, Nicco is innocent. That's been proven."

"Innocent of that murder, but not of everything." He pats the file as if to put an invisible exclamation mark on the point he's trying to drive home to me. "I'm going to dig deeper so I can convince you of that."

"You never will. I want to have some say in my own destiny. I deserve that. Six more months."

"It's too dangerous." He sighs, which gives me a sliver of hope. "We both know it."

"Three months then."

"The most I can give you is a week."

I will relish this small victory, but a week is not enough. Still, it is a start and proves Grayson isn't a tyrant after all. "That's not much time to relocate."

"No, it isn't, but it is necessary. The team has worked hard to set up your new identity."

"What's the new name?"

"Russell Jones."

"Not a fan of that. Where?"

"Alaska."

"Damn it, Grayson. You know I hate cold weather." I stand, feeling heady from my last win with him. "I'm not going there. Find somewhere else."

"There is nowhere else, Josh. Maybe later, but right now we have to move."

"No." Daring to push so that I can spend just a little more time with Nicco, I clear my throat. "One month. That's final."

"I love how you always try to negotiate your way through these changes, but understand there's nothing final about any of this until I say so." He smiles, which only fuels my frustration.

"I'm not your prisoner anymore. We're doing this my way from now on."

"Have you forgotten about your grandparents and your sister? That's why you're here. To protect them."

"Damn it, you can be so cruel sometimes." I exhale, realizing I've lost once again. This is my hell, and he's the devil in charge. Through the smoke and flames of this terrible life, I get glimpses of memories from my past. The car accident that took my parents' lives when I was just five. My loving grandparents, who raised my baby sister and me. Birthdays, when Grammy made my favorite cake, Double Fudge Chocolate. Fishing trips with Pappy. Holding Jenny's hand on the way to school. And so many more, each wonderful and painful, reminders of all I've lost.

Because of Grayson's protocols, I never got a chance to say good-bye.

"They're safe, Josh." He sucks on his unlit cigar. "Because you keep doing the right thing. And the *right thing* right now is you need to get the hell out of Dallas. The Southside mob believes you're dead."

"So does my family."

Manufacturing the story of my supposed death was Grayson's idea. His superiors didn't go for the idea at first, but one talent the man has is how relentless he can be when he believes he's doing the right thing. Once he got the approval, he went to work. All it took for the lie to take hold was switching my dental records with a John Doe who drowned in Lake Michigan. Not sure how he got that done, but he did. To the entire world, the person I was is dead.

"Your family is alive because of that belief. Let's keep it that way."

I stand, accepting my defeat. "Okay. You win. One week."

I'm no closer to solving my problems than I was when I got here. I don't want to leave, but Grayson is right. I have to protect my family and my friends. *And Nicco.*

I PARK in my spot at Mockingbird Place and notice two things. One, Nicco's parking spot is empty. Where could he be? Two, a guy in a dark jacket next to a black Mustang is snapping photos with his phone. Who is he and how did he get inside the gate? A person has to have a clicker to get into the parking lot or the code to get through the walk-in gate.

"Hey, do you mind if I ask you a question?" He starts walking my direction.

"Sure," I answer, trying to sound calm. I'm always uneasy with strangers. It's no wonder, given my history.

"You're with Red Shimmer, right? Josh White?"

Just a fan. This only proves that Grayson is right. I'm too exposed here. Damn it.

"Yes, I am. Who are you?"

"My friends call me 'Digs.'"

"How did you get inside the gate, Digs?"

He shrugs. "Sorry. I just waited for someone to drive out and I came in before the gate closed."

Fan or stalker? How long has he been watching me? "You shouldn't have done that."

"I know. I know. Sorry. I'll leave, but could I get a picture first?"

"Sure, but then you must leave, okay?"

"I will. I promise." He comes over and leans close to me. "Say cheese."

"Cheese."

"One more?"

"No." I step away. "You need to go, Digs. Now."

"Okay. Okay. Thanks Josh. You don't know how much this helps me out." Digs hurries to his Mustang.

I stay put, making sure he drives off the property.

Once the gate closes, I rush into the apartment.

Where is Nicco? Shouldn't he be through with his shift by now? Seeing my note from this morning in a place other than where I left it lets me know he must have read it. But there's no note from him. No text message. Nothing.

Why am I letting that bother me? I've got to leave in a week.

And then a dark thought enters my mind. What if *they* have him?

Oh, God, no!

I bring out my cell and call Nicco's number.

icco

MOM and I sit in the ICU waiting room, a space of bright colors with side tables filled with magazines meant to disguise its real purpose. This is the place where people anxiously await news of their loved one's condition.

"Mom, I need to call the office to let them know why I'm late."

She nods absentmindedly, picking up a copy of a magazine about gardening that has to be at least two years out of date.

I bring out my phone.

"McBain Charters and Pilot School, how may I help you?"

"Liza, this is Nicco." I quickly fill her in on what happened since I left.

"That's terrible. I know Mrs. Clark," she says.

"I'm not surprised. Probably everyone in Dallas does in one way or another."

As Liza tells me about the first time she met Mrs. Clark, I look at the clock, anxious for an update. Stephen and Tony are with her now. We're all thankful that Maddox was on call. He's working with the ICU doctors on her case. We are still waiting to hear from him about her condition.

"She was so good to my mother." Liza's voice shakes with emotion. "Mrs. Clark came every day to pray with her during the chemo treatments. It meant the world to my mother. She's been cancer free for ten years now. I'll let her know about Mrs. Clark. I'm sure she'll want to come and pray with her."

"I'm sure she'd like that." I can hear the strain in my own voice.

"Nicco, Mrs. Clark is tough."

"Yes, she is." I remember the second week after I got out of prison and the dear lady requested my help delivering meals for the elderly. She had so much energy and life. I had trouble keeping up. "As soon as the doctors tell us about her prognosis, I will head back if that's okay."

"Of course it's okay. Stay with your family. I've got the office covered. The phone only rang twice since you left, and one of those was a wrong number. It's slow. Take the rest of the day off."

I hear the beep letting me know I have another call coming in. I glance at my phone's screen. *It's Josh.* Needing to hear his voice, I want to click over as quickly as possible. "Thanks, Liza. I'll see you tomorrow."

"You got a deal."

The call ends.

"Hey, Josh."

"Hi, Nicco." His voice has a comforting and calming impact on me. "Just wondering if you're going to be home for dinner tonight."

"I'm not sure." I take a deep breath, hating to deliver the bad news but knowing I must. "Mrs. Clark had a stroke."

"Oh, no. Sweet Mrs. Clark from the church?"

"Yes, I was having lunch with my mom, Stephen, and Tony. Then Stephen got a call that she had suffered a stroke. We're all at the hospital now waiting to hear from Maddox about her condition."

"I'll notify S & M and then I'll be right over."

"Okay. She's in ICU room 14, and we're in the waiting room. Stephen, being clergy, can go in anytime, but the rest of us can only go in once an hour."

"I certainly understand but I'm still coming," he says firmly, which thrills me more than I imagined it would.

I need him.

"Can I bring you anything?" Josh asks.

"I think we're good. Just glad you're coming." I put my phone away.

"Do you have to go?" Mom puts down the magazine she'd picked up to pass the time.

"No. Liza is going to cover for me." I see Stephen and Tony come through the double doors that lead to where Mrs. Clark was taken.

They sit down across from us.

"Is she okay?" I ask, fearing the worst.

"She's hanging in there," Tony tells us. "Maddox and the other doctors are in with Mrs. Clark now."

"The nurses told me we should know something pretty quick." Stephen is still clearly shaken.

"I spoke with Josh and he is going to notify S & M," I tell them. "He's on the way now and I expect S & M will be right behind him."

"No doubt." Tony grabs Stephen's hand. "Sweetheart, how about a cup of coffee?"

He shakes his head. "Thanks, honey, but I want to stay right here."

"Of course. Whatever you need." Tony's full attention is on Stephen, which is no surprise. Their bond is undeniable and unshakable. It's good that they have each other during this kind of crisis.

I look up and see Jaris walk into the waiting room. He's Maddox's husband as well as the other doctor at Mockingbird Place. Our two MDs live in Unit H.

I wave at him. "Over here, doc."

In jeans and T-shirt instead of his usual scrubs, Jaris steps over to us. "Maddox sent me a text about Mrs. Clark. Any news yet?"

We shake our heads.

"Let me go see what I can find out." He walks to the ICU.

"I've always liked his take-charge attitude," Mom says.

Stephen smiles weakly. "Me, too."

He, Tony, Mom, and I stare at the double door, waiting. It reminds me of how slow time can tick by. Only five minutes have passed since Jaris left us, yet it feels like the clock has stopped.

Sarah and Martha rush into the waiting room. For women in their late seventies, they can move very fast, but I suspect this hyper-speed has more to do with adrenaline than anything else. The worry in their eyes cannot be missed.

"Any news yet about Julia?" Martha takes the seat next to me.

"Still waiting to hear," Stephen answers in an anxious tone. "Jaris just went back to talk with Maddox. He said he would be right out with info for us."

Sarah sits down next to Stephen. "Stephen, this would be a good time for a prayer."

"S, I totally agree." Martha looks at Stephen. "We could all use a little encouragement from above right now."

"I know I could." It's obvious to me that S & M see how upset we all are, especially Stephen. Having him pray might help calm all of us. "Do you mind, Stephen?"

"Of course not. Let's join hands."

We gather in a circle and close our eyes.

"God of all comfort, our only help in time of need: We humbly beseech thee to behold, visit, and relieve thy sick servant Julia Clark for whom our prayers are desired. Look upon her with the eyes of thy mercy; comfort her with a sense of thy goodness; Restore her to health, and...and...and..." Stephen's voice cracks with emotion.

I open my eyes and see Tony put his arm around him.

Tony begins the prayer and we all join in. "Our Father who art in heaven..."

It helps to calm us, but I feel my heart breaking. Under my

breath I whisper, "God, please. Don't take her. I know she's lived a long life, but we still need her. We're not ready for her to go."

When we open our eyes, we discover Jaris and Maddox standing near us.

"We came in during the prayer." Jaris turns to Maddox. "He has news for us."

"Mrs. Clark is stable."

"Thank God," Stephen whispers.

"It was very smart of her to call 9-1-1 because of the headache." Maddox continues filling us in on her prognosis. "I'm keeping her until we know more about her condition. That may take twenty-four hours, a week, or longer."

"Can we see her?" I ask.

"Yes, but understand she's been through quite the ordeal. She needs rest. Her headache is better, but you'll see that her speech is slightly slurred, a symptom of the stroke."

My gut tightens. "Will that be permanent?"

"Sometimes it can be and sometimes it goes away. We'll just have to wait and see. There is a risk that she could have another stroke, especially at her advanced age. The blood thinners should reduce that risk, but she's not out of the woods yet."

All my years in prison never prepared me for this. My eyes are stinging from the tears I'm holding back. I repeat my earlier prayer, asking God to spare Mrs. Clark. I didn't realize how much she meant to me until now. I might lose her. These bonds of friendship with her and these wonderful people may have only begun since I was released, but they are strong and forever.

I look up and see Josh walk into the waiting room. I step over to him and he puts his arms around me and I hug him back. No words. Not necessary. Somehow, we both know what the other is feeling.

Someone touches my shoulder and I look up. It's Harvey and Nathan.

They both put their arms around us.

"We're going to pull through this," Harvey says. "We always do."

Nathan nods. "I hope you're feeling hungry. We have caterers bringing enough food for everyone. Besides the rest of our gang, I'm sure there'll be quite a few members from Stephen's church showing up."

As if on cue, several people from the church walk into the waiting room, anxious to hear news about Mrs. Clark. Stephen and our two docs go over to them to bring them up to date on her current prognosis.

Josh and I move to the far end of the room to make space for the crowd of supporters showing up for Mrs. Clark.

"Funny how our Mockingbird Place family always brings food in a crisis," I whisper to Josh. "It might seem strange to most, but you know how it is with our neighbors. When in a crisis, we come together to support each other."

"Always." Josh takes a deep breath.

I notice him clenching his hands. "Are you okay?"

"Yeah, under the circumstances."

"She's has the best doctors, Josh."

"I know she does. I just…just need a breath of fresh air." Without another word, he walks out of the waiting room.

"What's up with Josh?" Nathan asks.

"I'm not sure." I rush to find him.

There's clearly more to his reaction than just worrying about Mrs. Clark. Did something happen at his meeting? Was it with Grayson?

Chapter 6

D^{igs}

I'M careful to stay back from Josh White's car. I don't want him to notice I'm following.

This is one of those jobs I hate, but I don't have a choice. I don't know why my buddies are so worried about Nicco. He's here. They've been in Chicago for years, which he doesn't even have a clue about. They just need to chill out. But they won't. Jaz, Duke, and Jose are like my brothers. I know them. They're tough but also way too nervous. They worry about every minor detail.

Ever since Nicco got out of prison, they've demanded I keep tabs on him. I have better things to do. If I didn't have to depend on them supplying me with drugs for my customers, I'd tell them all to go to hell, friends or not.

Josh White is Nicco's new roommate. I'm going to find some dirt on him that I can use as leverage against Nicco that will give me the upper hand. Once Nicco is under my control, I'll be able to convince my friends to let me off the hook.

My phone buzzes. It's Jaz.

"What's up, bud?"

"That picture you sent of Nicco's roommate. When did you take it?"

"Just a little bit ago. Why?"

"You know who he is?"

"Yeah. Josh White. He's a big deal in the local music scene."

"Oh, he's a lot more than that, Digs, and his real name isn't Josh White."

"What do you mean?"

"Just keep your eyes on him. You may have just found our winning lottery ticket."

Chapter 7

J *osh*

WALKING OUT OF THE HOSPITAL, I feel very sad. Seeing all the outpouring of love and concern for Mrs. Clark reminds me of everything I'll be giving up in a week. When I hugged Nicco, I forgot for a moment that I have to leave for Alaska. I wanted to hold on to him and never let go. It felt so right, like I belonged in his arms for the rest of my life.

"Josh, hold up." Nicco rushes up behind me, ripping my heart apart. "You're not leaving, are you?"

"How did you find out that I was leaving?" I snap back. I should push him away as fast and hard as I can. It's the only way I can ensure he'll be safe.

He shrugs. "You seemed upset and now you're holding your car keys."

Realizing we are on two different wavelengths, I glance at the keys in my hand. *He didn't find out about me leaving. He doesn't know anything. Thank God.*

Softening my tone, I say, "I guess I was on autopilot when I pulled them out of my pocket."

"Are you going back to our apartment or can you come back inside? The caterers should be here any minute. I think food would be good for all of us."

Why does he have to be so perfect and thoughtful? "Sure thing. I'll come back in after I get a little more air."

"Would you like some company? I could use some air too."

I should say "no" and send him away. That's the right thing to do. But I can't. I want to spend as much time with Nicco as I can before Alaska and the new identity Grayson is giving me. This feels so familiar. Running. It's been my life since the murder.

"You okay, Josh?" His eyes lock on mine. "Is something wrong?"

"Nothing's wrong. Just daydreaming, I suppose. Yes. I'd like for you to stay with me to get some fresh air."

"Good, because if you're trying to get rid of me, that's simply never going to happen." He leans over and kisses me.

He pulls me in close, and I deepen our kiss.

It's wonderful. I've never felt such a connection with just a kiss before. But I do now. Our tongues tangle together and passion rises inside me. This is what I've always wanted, but I know I'm setting myself up for heartbreak. *I'm out of control and can't help myself.*

Nicco smiles. "Damn, you sure do know how to kiss."

"Oh, you think so, do you?"

"Perhaps we should get that fresh air you wanted and you could teach me more on lipology, Professor White."

I feel the gray mood inside me melting away. I take his hand and hold out my keys. "Follow me, student Mantonvani. I know just the place."

As fast as I can, I lead him to my car.

I grin. "Welcome to my classroom."

We jump inside and begin kissing and hugging each other until the windows fog.

"I'm getting the hang of it, Professor, but I think more private tutoring is needed, don't you agree?"

I laugh. "You deserve an A-plus on today's pop quiz, but I would be happy to accommodate your studies to ensure you graduate with honors."

"Honors? I want to be Valedictorian."

Our phones buzz.

Finding a sliver of self-control, I release him and lean back. "Normally I would say we should ignore texts messages, but under these circumstances, we better see who it is."

"You're right." Nicco quickly presses his lips to mine once again and then brings out his phone to read the text. "Harvey says the food has arrived."

"I'm hungry, how about you?"

"Starving."

"We better get back then."

As we walk to the waiting room, I think how wonderful the last few minutes were with Nicco. I want more. Need more. Everyone believes I'm a player, but I'm not. I'm sure Nicco is aware of my reputation. I wish I could let him know the *real* me, but I can't. Besides, if he thinks I'm just a player, that's a good thing, isn't it? I definitely don't want to hurt him. I'll make it clear that this is just casual fun. With my rep, I'm sure it will be an easy sell. Besides, it seems to me like that's what he's wanting from the playfulness we had in the parking lot. If he's not into the *friends-with-benefits* thing, then *friends-without-benefits* will have to suffice—friends for my last week in Dallas at least.

I know I'm playing with fire, but if I can stay in control, no one will get burned. I just want to enjoy my last few days with him. That's not asking too much. When I'm isolated in frozen Alaska with only Grayson to talk to, I can still have my dreams of this wonderful man to get me through the long winter's nights. Of course, I will also always wonder what might have been under different circumstances. We might have had a chance at a real future...together. I'm fooling myself, aren't I? There's one person who will get burned, and that's me. My heart is going to break in two.

"Josh, be careful." Nicco's warning brings me back to the present.

I stop. He's pointing at a mop bucket full of water that I was about to step into.

I sigh. "That would have been quite a mess. Thanks for saving me."

"You must have been way out there in your thoughts." He places his hand on my shoulder, leading me around the obstacle. "They even have the orange cones around it."

"I was in deep thought imagining how tasty Harvey and Nathan's catered food is going to be."

"Let's go eat."

I nod and we walk into the waiting room with all our friends. As I fill my plate with the food, Nicco's words of caution swirl in my mind over and over. *"Josh, be careful."*

I glance at him and he smiles back at me.

I don't want to be careful, Nicco. I only have a few days left with you. I want to taste your lips again. I want to feel your body next to mine. Damn it, I want to hold onto you until this nightmare vanishes, until nothing is left but you. It won't be real, and it won't last, but for a few precious moments I can pretend this is forever.

Chapter 8

N*icco*

AFTER JOSH and I fill our plates, we take a couple of seats next to S & M.

"I doubt most hospitals would allow anyone to bring in a catered meal to a waiting room," Sarah says.

Martha nods. "Yes, but this one definitely bends the rules for Harvey."

"He is a huge donor, after all," Josh adds.

I know the small talk is just a way for us to ease our worry about Mrs. Clark.

Franki and Chad rush in.

Josh stands, placing his unfinished meal on the seat. "I'll be back. Need to fill them in on Mrs. Clark's status."

"Go. I'll protect your meal."

He smiles.

As I watch him approach Franki and Chad, I start thinking

43

about the fun we had in the parking lot. He really turns me on. How easy it would be to fall for him. I loved the closeness I felt when we kissed. But something is not right. I just can't put my finger on it. The way he nearly bit my head off when I first caught up with him was very strange. Then he completely changed. I took a chance when I kissed him, but man, the way he kissed me back blew my mind. I'm so excited about my future lessons in lipology with Professor White.

"What are you smiling about, Nicco?" Martha asks.

"M, don't be silly," Sarah says with a grin. "It's obvious he's smiling about Josh. Things must be going very well. I knew them moving in together was a good idea."

"Well, Nicco? Is S right? Are things going well between you two?"

If anyone else had asked me such a pointed question, I might have been a little irritated, but not with these two wonderful women. They are like mothers, with a little Cupid's heart mixed in, and want the best for all of us.

"I'd say that things between me and Josh are...well...are...he's a good roommate."

"Uh, huh." Martha winks. "I suspect that it's more than that, Mr. Niccolo Mantonvani."

Sarah says, "M, that's enough. Nicco and Josh will tell us when they're ready, which I'm certain won't be very long."

Before I can respond, Maddox rushes into the waiting room.

"Father Stephen, please come with me." Maddox's tone lets all of us know that something is very wrong with Mrs. Clark.

"Anthony, please come with me," Stephen says to my brother.

Tony nods and the three of them run to the ICU.

All our eyes are fixed on the double doors Stephen and Maddox went through. Not a single person utters a sound.

Josh leads my mom to me. They each take seats, placing me between them.

Mom puts her arm around my shoulder and Josh takes my hand. When I look at him, I see tears brimming in his eyes. I feel myself getting choked up but I must be strong for Josh.

Around us are our friends and the church members who are also comforting each other.

After several silent minutes, Stephen and Tony come back into the room.

We surround them to hear the news.

"Mrs. Clark passed away quietly just a moment ago." Stephen's voice shakes with grief, a grief I share with him and my brother. "Tony and I were holding her hands as she went to be with the Lord. There will be no more suffering for her."

Tears flow freely from the crowd as Stephen leads us in another prayer. I close my eyes, choking back my own pain. Mrs. Clark accepted me. God, I will miss her. But I have to be strong for Tony and Stephen, for everyone. They'll need me.

I feel Josh take my hand. I squeeze his hand gently, keeping my eyes closed. His touch draws out a single tear from me. What is it about him that causes my walls to crumble and allows me to feel?

As Stephen's prayer comes to a close, I wipe the tear away with my free hand.

JOSH, Tony, Stephen, and I walk into Unit G.

"Have a seat, guys," Josh says. "I'll open a bottle of wine."

I nod. "I'll get the glasses."

"Thanks. I'll definitely need wine for this." Stephen holds the folder Mrs. Clark prepared with him. Inside are her instructions on what she wanted for her funeral. "The reading of her will won't be for another month. According to her attorney, she left something for the church and also for everyone at Mockingbird Place."

I hand him a glass of wine. "Are you serious?"

He nods. "That's how she is…she was."

Tony takes Stephen's hand. "I bet we'll each get some kind of memento to remember her by. She thought of us as her family."

Stephen takes a sip of wine. "She and her late husband never had children."

"I remember one conversation I had with her when she brought her weekly cookies to me," Josh says, taking the seat next to mine. "She called us her boys and girls."

"After you became rector," Tony says to Stephen, "she became a fixture around here."

"She's been in my corner from day one. When a few of the members objected to having a gay priest, she not only scolded them but she completely turned them around. Now they are some of the most faithful members of our church."

"She was charming, that's for sure." Josh wipes his eyes. "It's amazing how much she's bonded with everyone at Mockingbird Place. I know S & M are crushed that she's gone."

Stephen pats the folder and his voice cracks. "How am I going to get through the service without losing it?"

Tony hugs him. "You'll do fine, sweetheart. I'll be there with you."

As tears fall from their eyes, I clench my jaw. I miss her so much, too, but I have to be strong for them. I need a distraction because I can't cry.

I leave my chair to compose myself.

"Where you going?" Josh asks.

"To get some tissues for you guys and to open another bottle of wine."

"Ah. Okay." His eyes narrow slightly.

Is he seeing through my charade? I'm not sure, but the task gives me just enough time to get my emotions under control. I return and hand the tissues to each of them. As they dry their eyes, I refill their glasses.

"I guess we better get started." Stephen opens the folder and looks at Josh. "The first thing she requested is for an old-fashioned wake at her home."

"We'll ask S & M to help organize that," Tony says.

I grin. "No one has better skills in that kind of thing than them."

"That's true." Stephen reads the next page. "Next, she asked Red Shimmer to sing the hymn you three wrote and performed on her last birthday."

"I'm sure Chad and Franki would be honored as much as I am."

"Excellent." Stephen hands a page to Tony. "Sweetheart, she wanted you to read theses passages at the service."

Tony silently reads the note from Mrs. Clark. "These verses are beautiful. I'm honored." He hands the page back to Stephen, who turns to me.

"She also hoped you would do her eulogy."

"Me? Why would she want me?"

"This is what she wrote. 'I would also like Niccolo Mantonvani to offer my eulogy. I can trust him to find the right words of comfort for my friends and family. He's strong and so capable."

Hold it together, Nicco.

I clear my throat, trying to keep my voice from breaking. "Of course, I'll do it."

Josh touches the back of my hand. "She's right, you know. You are strong and capable."

"Thanks." I leave my chair again.

Josh stares at me. "Where are you going now?"

Chapter 9

J *osh*

"I'LL BE RIGHT BACK." Nicco walks away from Stephen, Tony, and me.

I watch him head upstairs.

"Tony, that brother of yours is quite tough." Stephen refills his glass.

"Yes, he is. He's been my rock my whole life."

"But he's hurting just as much as we are, guys," I say. "He needs to let it out."

"That's not his way, Josh." Tony sighs. "I've never seen him shed a tear."

"Well, I think it's time he did." I stand. "I'll be right back."

I walk up the stairs and find Nicco on his bed, staring blankly at the wall. "Are you okay?"

He blinks and looks at me. "Sure. I'm fine."

"Really? You don't seem fine."

He shrugs. "Just thinking about giving the eulogy. I want to do Mrs. Clark justice."

"Come on, Nicco. It's more than that. You know it's okay to let your feelings out. You cared as much for her as the rest of us. We've shed tears. Why can't you?"

He stares at me for a moment, giving me hope that I'm getting through to him. But then he looks away and stands.

"We need to get downstairs and finish this planning session with Stephen and Tony." He walks out of the room.

"Damn it, Nicco. You don't have to be everyone's rock all the time."

My cell buzzes. I see it's a text from Grayson.

"We need to talk."

I text back, *"Later."*

I walk back downstairs.

After another hour and several phone calls, the plans for Mrs. Clark's wake and funeral are finalized. S & M happily agreed to host the wake. Franki and Chad agreed with me about us performing Mrs. Clark's birthday hymn. The wake will be tomorrow night at Mrs. Clark's home, and the funeral service is set for the very next day at the church.

"Thanks for all your help, guys." Stephen takes Tony's hand. "We couldn't have done it without you."

"There's a lot more to do the next couple of days, Stephen," Nicco says. "And I will be there for you and Tony the whole way, okay?"

"You're always there for me, bro." Tony hugs him.

I place my hand on Stephen's shoulder. "Whatever you need, I'm here for you too, guys."

"Thanks. We'll see you tomorrow."

They walk out.

Nicco shuts the door. "That was a productive planning session, don't you think?"

"Productive planning session? Is that what you call it?" I pick up my guitar and play a couple of chords. "Wouldn't it be nicer to say planning Mrs. Clark's wake and funeral?"

"It means the same thing, doesn't it?" He moves right next to me.

"Yes, but the way you say it sounds like a reporter on television reciting a few facts instead of someone who cared about her."

"What's bothering you, Josh?"

"We just spent the last hour talking about burying a woman who means so much to all of us, and you are acting like it's only a project to get through, a task to finish. Why are you being so hard? I know you're hurting, but you won't let your guard down. What exactly are you afraid of, Nicco?"

"I'm not afraid of a damn thing. What about you, Josh? What are you afraid of?"

I step back. "I don't know what you're talking about."

He steps forward. "Sure you do. What about all those texts that were coming in that you refused to answer? Why did you snap at me in the parking lot of the hospital earlier? I know something is wrong. I'm not an idiot."

"Fine. You're not an idiot. Let's drop it." I turn to flee this Pandora's box that we've just opened.

He grabs my arm. "No, you don't. You're not running away from me. Talk to me, Josh. What's really going on? Is it about that Grayson creep?"

"I can't tell you. Please, just let it go. It's too dangerous."

He pulls me in close. "I don't care how dangerous it is. You don't have to face it alone. I'm here for you. Don't you get that?"

He kisses me deeply, and I feel an overwhelming passion for him.

I stare into his eyes, wishing with all my heart things could be different. "I want to tell you so badly, Nicco, but I just can't. Please try to understand."

"Okay, sweetheart. But you will eventually tell me. Trust me."

"I trust you. I really do. This is not about trust." I press my lips to his, needing more of him. "Tonight, I just want to forget everything except you and me. Understand?" I kiss him again to make my point clear.

The way he kisses me back gives me his answer. His lips are full of heat and emotion.

"Fuck, you smell so good."

"It's just my aftershave," I tease. "I can go get it to show you. It's in the bathroom."

He laughs. "Not a chance. I want to see all of you, Josh."

"Funny, because I was just thinking the same thing."

We strip off our clothes, tossing them to the floor.

Having seen Nicco in the pool before, I knew his body was ripped. But standing next to him and touching every inch of his body, I'm amazed at the sheer male beauty he possesses. The ink on his arms and chest only adds to his masculinity, which pours out of him like hot steam from a locomotive.

I take a step back to get a better look at him. "Damn, Nicco. You're... you're... Just damn."

"I'll be whatever you want me to be, sweetheart."

"Just be yourself. That's all I want."

"That's all I want from you too." He steps up to me and we kiss slowly, our tongues and breaths becoming one.

I feel his cock pressing against me. Wrapping my fingers around his thickening shaft, I feel him grab my cock, which is throbbing, hardening, and stretching out. Like two wild beasts, we devour each other, sucking on each other's neck and fisting each other's dicks. Each wave of heat piles on top of the previous, causing my pulse to beat faster and my temperature to go higher.

"Fuck, you're smoking hot." His warm breath skates over my skin, sending electricity through my body.

I nuzzle Nicco's neck, inhaling his scent, which is a mix of steel and spice with a hint of the bees' nectar. "You smell so good, honey."

This moment with him is like no other I've ever experienced before. So freeing. So consuming. So alive. Nothing else exists. Not the past or the future. Just now. With him.

"Get on your knees, sweetheart," Nicco growls low, his lips grazing my ear. "I want to feel your lips on me."

As his overwhelming power and masculinity wrap around my own desires, I lick my way down his hard body, taking my time to enjoy the taste of him.

When I am down on my knees on the floor and facing his beast, I feel a delicious tremble move up and down my spine. I kiss the tip of his cock. The salty drop resting on his slit tempts me. I lick it, relishing the taste of it on my tongue. His lusty groans whet my own appetite.

As I swallow his thick length, I cup his balls and fist my own hard cock.

When I feel him tug on my hair, my toes curl. I bob up and down on him like a man possessed. I want him to come inside my mouth. I want to swallow every drop of his essence.

"Damn, that's so fucking good. Don't stop, sweetheart. Don't ever stop."

Escalating my attack, I swallow more of him, squeezing his balls slightly.

"Oh, God. Yes. Yes. I'm so close."

I'm close too. As my lips slide up and down his shaft, my hand pumps my cock at the same tempo. Faster and faster. Up and down. Squeezing. Sliding.

"Ohhh…fuuuck!" He pulls my hair hard, and I love it.

When his cream hits the back of my throat, I come with such force it takes my breath away. As I swallow every one of his savory drops, I glance up at him.

Nicco still holds my hair tight. His eyes are closed. His body shudders. He's the most beautiful sight I've ever seen.

I slowly release his cock. "That was so good."

He pulls me off the floor. "No, that was fucking fantastic, and I'm not done with you yet, sweetheart."

I grin. "You're not? What did you have in mind?"

He lifts me into his arms and winks. "I've been dreaming about this for a very long time. I'd rather surprise you."

As he carries me up the stairs, I lean my head into his shoulder. I can't remember ever feeling this way with anyone. Though I know it's impossible, I wish this night with him could last forever.

Chapter 10

J *az*

I'M TRYING my best to keep my cool, but walking into a prison with a hit man is nerve-racking.

Despite Baby Malone's small stature and foolish nickname, the man is ruthless and deadly. Because of his unusual practice of buying a new piece of jewelry after each hit, Baby drips in diamonds and gold.

Every step we take to the visitors' lounge, I keep feeling like any second one of the guards is going to grab me and throw me in a cell. Hell, I'm lucky I'm not in here. I've committed murder and a whole bunch of other crimes that would earn me life without parole. Unlike the man we've come to see this morning, I'm too smart and careful to get caught.

We walk into the lounge, taking a seat at one of the empty tables.

"I'll do the talking," Baby says.

"Whatever you say." I can't believe I'm about to see the infamous Teddy Thompson.

He may not have been smart enough to stay out of here, but he still runs a lot of things on the outside, though few know it. Unlike Clyde Walker, who's a pussy in my mind, Thompson leads with an iron fist. No one dares to cross him.

That's what I want. Respect. And money. And I'm about to get tons of both. Like I said before, the only difference between Thompson and me—I won't get caught. I'd never survive in here.

The door opens. The guards lead the inmates into the room.

Baby motions to Thompson.

He walks over to our table, glaring at me. "What the fuck, Baby? Who is this asshole?"

"Jaz Marino. You remember." Baby, who has always been steel whenever I've been with him, suddenly seems nervous. "He and his two buddies came from Dallas and joined the organization ten years ago."

"Yeah. He's one of our grunts. Why the fuck did you bring him here? You know I don't want anyone else at these meetings."

"Hold on, boss. You'll want to see what he has. It's important."

"It damn well better be." Thompson sits down across from me. "Show me."

I bring out Digs' photo of Josh White. "Do you recognize him, Mr. Thompson?"

His eyes widen. "Yes, I recognize this fucker. He's the asshole whose testimony put me in here. But he's dead. Why the fuck are you showing me a photo of a dead man?"

"No, sir. He's not dead. My friend Digs took this photo of him this morning in Dallas."

"No fucking way." Thompson turns to Baby. "This for real?"

He nods.

A crooked smile crosses Thompson's face. "This is very good news."

"I told you, boss."

Feeling elated, I say, "He's going by the name of Josh White and performs in a band called Red Shimmer."

Thompson stabs his finger into the photo of Josh White. "I'm coming for you, asshole. Finally, I'll get my revenge." He turns to Baby. "Let's initiate the plan to get me out of here."

"Way ahead of you, boss. Things are already in motion."

"What did you say your name was?" Thompson asks me.

"Jaz Marino, sir."

"Baby, give him a bonus. He's earned it."

icco

WHEN THE EARLY morning sunlight comes through my shades, I slowly and quietly get out of the bed. Josh continues breathing softly, so I know I didn't disturb his sleep.

Before going downstairs to get the coffee made, I take a long look at him tangled in my sheets. He's the man I want. But if I didn't know it before, I know it now. I'm deeply in love with him and want him in my life forever. Whatever I have to do to convince him we belong together, that's what I'm going to do.

I go downstairs, wondering when would be the right time to confess my feelings to him. I want him to know so that I can help him with whatever problem he's facing. As I turn on the coffeemaker, I hear my phone buzzing on the counter. I left it downstairs after Josh and I ripped off each other's clothes.

"Hello?"

"Nicco. Thank God you're okay." Gage's voice comes through loud and clear, reminding me of our dinner plans last night.

"Gage, I'm so sorry. I totally forgot about dinner. A good friend of mine passed away."

"Oh. I didn't know."

"Liza didn't tell you?"

"I haven't seen her. I didn't get back from Vegas until late. She was already gone. I went straight to the restaurant for our date."

It's obvious now that the dinner wasn't about my job. He's interested in me. "Gage, I'm sorry I didn't show but I need to make something clear to you. I like working with you and being your friend but...I'm in a relationship now." *With Josh.*

"You are? When? You were single just yesterday."

"It's new but very important to me. I hope you understand."

"Sure. Good for you. I'll see you later today at the office and you can tell me all about it."

"Actually, I need a couple of days off for the wake and funeral."

"Oh. Okay. I'll see you day after tomorrow then."

"Thanks, Gage. I appreciate it."

"You got it, buddy. And if things don't work out with your new friend, I'd still like to buy you that steak sometime."

I laugh. "You're too much, Gage. Talk to you later."

"Bye."

I lean against the counter and smile. I'm happy. Really happy. Because of Josh.

I hear him scream, and shockwaves go through my entire body. I race upstairs to save him.

He's flailing on the bed, punching into the air. "Stop it. Don't hurt them. I'm the one to blame. Take me."

I grab one of his wrists and he swings at me, landing a punch on the side of my face.

I shake him. "Josh, wake up. You're having a nightmare. Wake up."

"What's going on?" His eyes open wide and he sits up, glancing wildly around the room. "Where are they?"

I put my arms around him. "No one is here but me, sweetheart. You're safe."

He leans his head into my shoulder. "That seemed so real."

"Just a nightmare, sweetheart. It's okay." I kiss his forehead. "Let's go downstairs. The coffee is ready and you can tell me all about it."

He leans back and looks at me. "It was just a bad dream. No big deal. Nothing to worry about."

I can feel him already pulling away. "Sorry, Josh. I don't believe you."

"Can we please just go have some coffee?" He puts on his robe and heads for the door. "You coming?"

"Yes, I'm coming, but this isn't over."

Josh races down the stairs and I follow.

He fills two cups with coffee, handing one to me and then adding cream and sugar to his.

He takes a drink. "Mm. Just what I needed. But I really am hungry after all that exercise we did together last night." He winks at me. "I'm in the mood for a big breakfast. Let's go to Aunt Lucy's for pancakes. What do you say?"

"I say you're stalling."

"Please, Nicco. Let's just go have breakfast. We need it after all we've been through."

"Okay, I'll go to breakfast with you, but like I said before—this isn't over." I lean over and kiss him.

His phone starts ringing upstairs.

"Same person who was texting you all night?" I ask.

"Maybe. I've got to get that, Nicco."

"Sure, and I need to get ready for *our breakfast date*," I say, trying to make it even clearer to him how I feel.

He smiles and we rush upstairs together.

I head into the bathroom and he walks into his bedroom. I leave the door open intentionally. I want to know that whomever is calling him isn't part of the trouble he's in.

"I'm here. Yes. That's none of your business, Grayson."

Grayson. I knew it.

I walk out of the bathroom and into Josh's room, ready to go to battle for him.

He holds up his hand to stop me, still talking into his phone. "I don't like it, but I know you're right. When? Okay, I'll be there." He puts his phone away and looks at me. "You shouldn't have been listening, Nicco."

"I care about you, Josh. Whatever Grayson has over you, I can help. You don't have to face that prick alone."

"You don't get it. This is my hell, not yours." He looks down. "I shouldn't have let things go as far as they did with you. It's my fault. I'm sorry."

"You can push and push and push. But I'm not going anywhere, understand?"

"But I am. Nicco, I haven't told anyone this. I'm leaving Dallas in a few days for good."

I feel my entire body tighten with anger. "With that bastard Grayson?"

His eyes lock with mine. "Yes."

Chapter 12

J*osh*

NICCO FROWNS and his face darkens, which crushes me. "You're lying, Josh. I know you."

He's right, but I can't admit it.

Time to act like a total asshole, Josh. "You know me? Then you also know I'm not someone who settles down with one guy. That's my rep, isn't it? I figured a little sidestep with Grayson would be nice. He's got money and wants to spend it on me. Why not? I'm young. I deserve some fun. Besides, I'm tired of this place. I need something new and fresh."

"You're telling me a bunch of bullshit. If you don't want to confide in me, fine. But don't ever lie to me again, understand?" He turns around and walks out, not waiting for me to respond.

With all my heart I want to go after him, but I know I can't. Damn it, this hurts so much.

A few minutes later, I watch a fully dressed Nicco walk down the stairs. He doesn't even look at me when he leaves out the door.

I've hurt him so bad. Fuck. I wish I could tell him the truth. He's the one man who I know would do anything for me. He's made that crystal clear. And I would do anything for him, including giving him up so he'll be safe. I love him.

God, I do love him.

Could there be another way? Damn it, Grayson. This isn't right.

I shake my head. "It isn't right. None of it. I didn't do anything wrong. I deserve better."

And then it hits me what I have to do.

Chapter 13

 N *icco*

STILL REELING from what happened with Josh, I get in my car and drive out of Mockingbird Place's parking lot. I don't have a destination. I just need time to clear my head.

What could be so terrible that Josh has to lie to me? I know the ugly underbelly of life. I've lived it. Doesn't he realize I can help him with whatever he's facing?

I turn on the radio to KCXC-FM because music usually works to calm me down and focus my mind. As I merge onto Central Expressway heading north, I listen to the lady finish the weather report.

"This weekend looks promising. Sunny skies and temperatures in the mid-70s. I'm Amanda Evans with your KCXC weather report. Back to you, Blake."

"Come on, Blake. Play something to help me," I say aloud, though I know my old roommate can't hear me.

"Thanks, Amanda." Blake's deep voice comes through loud and clear. "I know I'm going to enjoy the wonderful weekend at Lee Park. Red Shimmer will be playing at the fundraiser that the Rainbow Coalition is sponsoring for runaway LGBT youths. For information or tickets, check out KCXC's website. Here's Red Shimmer's most requested song of the week, with Josh White singing lead. This is 'On the Run.' "

As the fast, pulsing beat of the song thumps in my ears, I squeeze the steering wheel tight. I listen to Josh sing the lyrics which are full of angst and frustration. With every verse, I feel my heart rate speeding up. One line makes my gut tighten. *"Don't try to follow me, I'm going too fast."*

"What are you running from, Josh?" I glance down at my speedometer and realize I'm going eighty-five, fifteen miles over the posted speed limit.

Damn.

I take my foot off the accelerator just as I see flashing red and blue lights in my rearview mirror. *Too late.*

Even though my record has been cleared of the murder, it's still not pleasant being pulled over. My experience with most law enforcement has actually been quite positive. The guards at the prison were professional. I did what was expected and they appreciated it. Made my life easier.

Getting out my license and registration, I roll down my window.

"Good morning, sir. Do you have an emergency?" The officer is about my age and has a warm voice.

"No, sir." I hand him my documents.

"Do you realize how fast you were going, Mr. Mantonvani?"

"I just realized I was speeding. I'd been listening to my roommate's band on the radio and was getting into the rhythm of it. When I looked down I was going eighty-five miles per hour."

"That's exactly what I clocked you at. What's your roommate's band?"

"Red Shimmer."

"Are you serious?" He smiles. "I love their music. I'm a big fan. I saw them play at the Stockyards a few months back and I'm going to their concert at Lee Park this weekend. So is your roommate Chad, Josh, or Franki?"

"Josh White."

"So was it one of the songs that he sings the lead?"

"Yes."

"Okay, don't tell me. Was it 'On the Run?' "

"How did you know?"

"Because of how fast your were going." He hands back my documents.

"I'm sorry, sir."

"Okay, I'm just going to give you a warning this time, but be sure not to have such a heavy foot when you're listening to Red Shimmer, okay?"

"I will be more careful. Thanks, Officer..."

"Mike Tucker. Hope to see you at the concert."

"I'll be there." *But will Josh, or will he already be gone?*

Officer Mike returns to his squad car. When he turns off the lights, I pull back into traffic with no answers to my problem of getting Josh to trust me. Should I go back and see if he's still willing to have breakfast with me? Or should I just go by myself so I can come up with something else to say to him? I just don't know what to do.

My fuel light comes on, letting me know I need gas. As I pull into a gas station, my phone rings. It's Tony.

I really could use his advice right now. "Hey, brother."

"Hey, I was just wondering if you wanted some help on Mrs. Clark's eulogy."

"I hadn't thought about that yet. Yes. I sure could use your help. And I also have something I need your advice on. Could you meet me at Aunt Lucy's Diner in about ten minutes? Breakfast will be my treat."

"Now you're talking my language. See you there."

After I fill my tank, I drive to the diner. Walking inside, I see my brother is already sitting at a booth.

"Hey," I say, sliding into the seat across from him. "Thanks for this."

"That's what brothers are for."

Lucy, the redheaded woman in her sixties who owns the place, comes up with two cups of coffee for us. "How are the Mantonvani brothers today?"

"We're good," Tony answers with a smile. "How about you?"

"I'm great, as usual. What else can I get you gentlemen?"

Tony hands her the menu. "I'm going to have the Blue Plate special. Eggs scrambled, bacon crispy, wheat toast, and hash browns."

"Same for me."

"I'll throw in a short stake of pancakes for both of you." She winks and walks away.

"You want me to help you with Mrs. Clark's eulogy first, or do you want to tell me what's bothering you about Josh?" Tony asks.

"How did you know I'm having trouble with Josh?"

"I'm your brother. The same way you know when things are bothering me. What's going on?"

Through our meal I give him every detail. About seeing Grayson at our door on the day I moved in with Josh. About how Josh and I played music together and the connection I felt with him. Then how he snapped at me in the hospital parking lot, only to quickly turn around and make out with me in his car.

"You've fallen in love with him, haven't you?" Tony has always been a guy who is direct to a fault.

"Yes. I have, but I can't get through to him. Something is very wrong and he won't share it with me. He's lying."

"About what?"

"Josh told me that he's moving out of Dallas to have a fling with this Grayson guy, but I know there's more to it than that. For one thing, he wouldn't leave Chad and Franki unless it was...was..."

"Was what?"

"It's got to be a life or death situation, Tony, or something just as bad."

"I agree with you. Stephen and I have noticed that something has been off with him for a while. We were thrilled when you decided to move in with him, thinking that would help. But obviously whatever the situation he's in is worse than any of us thought. Do Chad and Franki know he's planning on leaving?"

"I don't think so, but he didn't tell me."

"You lost your temper with Josh, didn't you?"

"Boy, you do know me, little brother. Yes, I did."

"What did that get you?"

"Not a damn thing."

"Okay, you wanted my advice, so this is what I think you should do. Go back home. Don't get mad. Just force the issue. I've known Josh for a long time. I'm sure he wants to tell you everything. Make it easy for him, Nicco."

"But I've tried that already."

Tony takes a sip of his coffee before responding. "Yes, you did. But you gave up and walked out mad."

"You're right."

"That's not like you. You never give up."

I smile. "I've never been in love before. I don't know how to act."

Tony leans across the table. "Love can be messy, brother, but you have to follow your heart."

"Right again. When did you get so smart?"

"I had a really good teacher in you."

Lucy walks up with a pot of coffee. "Refills, boys?"

"Yes, please," Tony says.

"Me, too. Thanks." As she walks away to help other customers, I take a sip. "Mm. They have the best coffee here. By the way, how's Stephen doing?"

"He's holding up but is overwhelmed with all the extra duties Mrs. Clark did around the church, which brings me to something I wanted to ask your advice about."

"I'll do my best for you. What is it?"

"I'm thinking about retiring from MMA fighting."

"I can tell you my answer right now. Yes. Retire. I'll be a lot less stressed worrying about you, and I bet I'll live longer too. Plus, you'll be leaving with an undefeated record. That's quite an accomplishment."

Tony shrugs. "There's a little more to it than that."

"Honestly, I'm surprised knowing how much you love what you do."

"I did love it, but I'm ready for the next chapter in my life with my wonderful husband. You know I've got a great deal of money saved, so I don't need a paycheck. I just want to help Stephen and the church. What do you think?"

"I think that's a fantastic idea." I've watched Tony's faith return. "You'll be perfect for the job, and I'm sure Mrs. Clark would be so pleased. Who knows? It might turn into a paying gig."

"I really don't care. My husband needs me. That's all that matters."

"You have my blessing. Go for it. I'm very proud of you, Tony."

Out of the corner of my eye, I see a man who I recognize walking straight to our booth.

The guy still wears the scar on his face I put there years ago. "Nicco, good to see you, buddy. When did you get out?"

I stand and place my fist on his chest. "None of your business, Digs. Now move, so me and my brother can get out of here."

"Sorry, I don't mean to bother you, but when I saw you I thought about an opportunity that has come up that I'd like to cut you in on. It would be like taking candy from a baby. What do you say?"

"No. Absolutely not."

"But it is such an easy score and with your expertise—"

"I said no. Now move."

"Not so fast, Nicco," Tony says. "I have some questions of my own."

Digs' eyes widen with fear when he recognizes my brother. His reaction doesn't surprise me one bit. Tony's size and demeanor are intimidating.

"You're little Tony. And you're also The Beast."

"I didn't know you were an MMA fan, Digs." Tony gets in the creep's face. "Where are your other buddies? The ones who let my brother take the heat and go to prison for a murder they committed?"

I realize what Tony's after. Justice. He wants the real killers, my so-called friends at the time, to pay for their crime and silence that kept me in prison for ten years.

"I wasn't there, Tony. Remember? It was Jaz, Duke, and Jose. They were the ones who killed your mother's boyfriend, not me." When Tony steps forward, Digs looks like he's about to melt into a puddle.

"You better tell me where they are now or I'll drag you outside and beat you to a pulp. You know I can do it."

"Okay. Okay. I'll tell you. All I know is they're all somewhere up north. Pittsburg, Chicago, maybe Boston. I don't for sure. I haven't seen or spoken to any of them for over a year. That's it. That's all I know. Please. Believe me."

I turn to Tony. I'm really proud of how he handles himself. "You got what you want?"

"For now." He glares at Digs. "Don't you dare tell your buddies about this, understand?"

"Yes. I get it. Sure. I swear. Just leave me alone."

"Get out of here," I tell the weasel. Seeing Lucy standing in the corner watching us, I add, "Don't ever come back here. Clear?"

"Yes, Nicco. I get it." Digs turns and runs out of the diner, like a rat seeking shelter.

I watch him get into a black Ford Mustang through the big windows.

"That's his fucking car. That son of a bitch has been stalking me for weeks."

Lucy walks up to us. "Very impressive, fellas. Thanks for not busting the guy up in here. Your breakfast is on me today."

"You don't have to do that," I say. "It was our issue, not yours."

She grins. "Mind your elders. Don't steal a lady's blessing."

"Thanks," Tony and I say in unison.

In the parking lot, my brother turns to me. "I don't believe that Digs just happened to walk into the diner and see you."

"That's how gangs work, Tony. Whenever someone gets out, they want to pull that person right back into the old life. Two reasons. One, it's another soldier in their army. Two, it keeps any info the former gang member might have out of the hands of the authorities. But Digs and anyone else who wants to recruit me is barking up the wrong tree. I'm done with that life."

"I know that. You were a kid yourself, and only trying to put food on the table for me and mom."

"You got a lot of info from Digs. So what's your plan?"

"I'm going to the DA right now with this new information. Do you think Digs will let those assholes know he saw us?"

"Maybe, but he was really scared."

"I'm going right now, so maybe we can get the jump on them before they have a chance to run."

I nod, as Josh's song *"On the Run"* plays in my head.

"Oh, I completely forgot that I was going to help you on the eulogy."

"Don't worry. I'll write it and you and Stephen can go over it with me later tonight after the wake. Right now, I want to get back to Josh. You understand?"

"I sure do. Good luck, brother."

When I pull into Mockingbird Place, I see Josh's parking spot is empty. He's gone. *Am I too late?*

Chapter 14

J *osh*

WITHOUT KNOCKING, I open Grayson's office door and find him sitting with his signature unlit cigar dangling from his lips.

"You're two hours early, Josh, but it's okay. I was able to get all your paperwork and ID documents ready quicker than I expected. I have us booked on the six PM flight to Anchorage tomorrow."

"Well, I hope you have a good flight by yourself because I'm not going." I lean over his desk. "I'm sick of this crap. I'm staying in Dallas and your people better protect my friends here and my family back home."

"We've been through this over and over. You know my hands are tied." He motions to the chair, but I remain standing.

"I'm not going anywhere. I have a career now and friends and —" My phone buzzes. It's a text from Nicco, asking where I am.

"You need to get that?"

I don't need to tell Grayson how I feel about Nicco. "Just do your job. That's all. Make it work. I'm not going to ping pong around the country anymore."

"This is more about your new roommate than anything else, isn't it?"

"So what if it is? I deserve a life. I deserve to be free. I deserve a chance at love."

Grayson clears his throat and puts the cigar in the clean ashtray. "I know this has been hard on you, Josh, but my superiors really want to move you just one more time."

"That's what you always tell me, and then I have to move again. 'This time, this place, it's the last, Josh.' Well, you're right this time. I'm staying. Make it happen."

He sighs. "You know the risks, Josh."

I slam my fists on his desk. "So do you. It's your job and your buddies in the United States Marshals Office to make sure I and everyone connected to me is protected. I'll say it again. I did my part. Now you do yours." I turn and walk out.

I haven't felt this sense of freedom since I had to disappear. I could see it in Grayson's eyes. He's going to come through for me. I know it. He's more than capable. Why didn't I stand up to him before now? Because I never had a good enough reason to. I smile, thinking about Nicco.

My phone buzzes.

Another text from Nicco. *"Where are you? We need to talk."*

I text back. *"Yes, we do. Where are you?"*

"Home."

What a wonderful word. One I haven't allowed myself to think about until Nicco.

I smile. *"On my way now."*

WHEN I WALK into the apartment, I see Nicco at the kitchen table writing something. "Hey, what are you working on?"

He glances at me. "Mrs. Clark's eulogy, but I can finish it later."

He slides the pen and papers to the side. "Right now, I want you to sit down and let's really have a heart-to-heart talk."

"Okay. That's what I want too." I sit down in the chair next to his. "I'm glad you said that because there's something I need to tell you." I sit next to him.

"Before you talk, there's something I need to tell you first." He takes my hand. "I love you, Josh. I told you to trust me before but you haven't. Hopefully knowing that I love you will change your mind. You can trust me with anything."

"I came here to tell you the truth about me because I do trust you. The truth is I want you, not just for a night but forever."

He leans back, releasing my hand. "But what about Grayson? What's up between you two?"

"That's as good a place to start as any I can think of. Grayson is a United States Marshal and is in charge of my case."

"Your case? What do you mean?"

"I'm in the witness protection program."

He looks shocked. "But I've been exonerated."

"No, Nicco. It's not about you. I've never gone to court about you."

He doesn't say anything for a few seconds, clearly processing everything I just told him. Finally, he says, "Of course it's not about me. That doesn't make sense. It was just my initial response. I guess I'm still adjusting to getting out of prison."

"It's okay. I understand."

"How long have you been in WITSEC?"

"So you know what that is?"

"In prison, you learn all the facets of the criminal justice system, including the federal witness protection program. What happened to you?"

"Seven years ago when I was only nineteen, I witnessed a double homicide. I was living in Chicago, pursuing my love of music. Me and three other guys formed a band. We were thrilled when one of the top producers in the area came to listen to us play. His name was Alec McTavish. He became our manager and everything seemed to be going up and up for us. A couple months after we signed with

Alec, we were headlining at one of the hottest clubs on the south side of the city. I couldn't have been happier. I thought my career was really going to take off. But what I didn't know was that Club Midnight Hour was run by Theodore Thompson."

Nicco frowns. "Teddy Thompson, the leader of the Chicago Southside mob?"

"The one and only. It was after two in the morning. My other bandmates had already taken off. Except for Alec, a lone bartender, and me, the place was empty." As I continue telling Nicco the story, I began to relive that horrible night.

"WHAT A NIGHT, ALEC," I said. "I've never dreamed it could be this good."

He smiled. "This is only the beginning, kid. Just you wait and see. I'm going take you places that will rock your world. Now, about that song that's been swirling in your head all day, how's that coming?"

"I think I've got it."

"Then you better write it down before you head out." He turns to the bartender. "Can we get a pen and some paper for this musical genius?"

"Sure thing, Mr. McTavish. Upstairs in the office. It's unlocked. Help yourself."

Alec smiled. "You heard him. Go."

I ran upstairs and found what I needed. When I started back downstairs, I saw three men with guns rush inside the club.

I bent down low on the landing and reached in my pocket for my phone, and then I realized I'd left it downstairs. Just then Teddy Thompson walked in and aimed his gun at the bartender. The poor kid begged for his life.

"Sorry, but we don't need any witnesses." The bastard shot him three times without a hint of humanity.

Thompson's men forced Alec to his knees.

The bastard pressed the barrel of his gun to Alec's forehead. "You've been holding back on me, McTavish, haven't you?"

"Teddy, I swear I've given you every cent."

"Don't bullshit me, asshole." Without another word, he blew Alec's head off.

After Teddy Thompson and his men left, I went downstairs with my legs

*shaking so hard I wasn't sure I would make it. I'd never been so scared in my
entire life. There was so much blood.*

I FEEL Nicco squeeze my hand, which brings me out of the
nightmare.

"What happened then?"

"I got my phone and called the police. From then on, things
went crazy. The authorities had been trying for years to get something on Teddy Thompson. They had always come up short until
they had me as a witness. After they arrested the murdering bastard,
they hid me until the trial. Everyone knew his reach was wide. Even
though my testimony helped send Thompson to prison, his lieu-
tenants searched for me because they wanted revenge. That's why I
was enrolled in the witness protection program. I was first sent to
Miami. Stayed there for only three months. Then I went to Oregon.
Then to Los Angeles. And on and on. Dallas is the place I've lived
the longest since this all began." I look at Nicco as the flood of
emotions I've been holding back finally let loose. "I lost everything
to protect my family and my friends. Everything, even my real
name."

"What is your real name, sweetheart?" he asks in a warm and
loving tone.

"Don't laugh."

He grins. "I won't."

"I was born Leroy Brown. You know...the song?"

"Oh, yeah. I've heard it plenty of times."

"Honestly, I prefer Josh White after all these years."

"Josh or Leroy...doesn't matter to me." He traces my jawline
with his hand. "So now I understand why you're supposed to move
out of Dallas. Grayson is trying to protect you."

He makes me feel like everything is really going to be okay. I've
never believed that before, until now. With him. With the man of
my dreams. Maybe it is just a dream, but I'm not willing to let it go.
Nothing matters but this moment with him.

"You can't imagine how many times I've moved or how many

different names I've had. But I'm done with it. I told this to Grayson just before I came home. I made it clear that he needs to protect my friends, my family, and me. That's his job."

"I wish I could have seen his face, but Josh—"

"No more buts. No more running. I want us to have a chance, Nicco. You and me." My whole world stands still and gets quiet. Am I wrong to pull him into my crazy, dangerous world? Of course I am. I've been selfish. But this isn't just about me anymore. It's about him. I want to make him happy, but at what cost?

He leans over and kisses me lightly. "I love you."

"I don't know what to say to that." With all my heart I want to say it back to him, but those three words from his lips seem to freeze time for me.

"You don't have to say anything, sweetheart." His reassuring smile melts away my insecurities and fear.

I put my arms around him and press my lips to his. It is like tasting bliss, heaven, and forever all wrapped up in hot desire. "Let's go to my room."

"You took the words right out of my mouth, sweetheart."

We rush upstairs, stripping out of our clothes every step of the way.

Like two crazy teenagers, we jump on the bed and into each other's arms.

Taking my face in his hands, Nicco kisses me full and deep. I put my arms around him, deepening the kiss. Our tongues tangle together as our hard cocks rub against each other below.

He licks a path down to my chest, biting at my nipples until they are hard and throbbing. I let my stare rove up and down his body that pro athletes would envy.

Nicco releases my nipple and looks at me, licking his lips. "Fuck, you're like a drug to me. I can't get enough of you, baby."

I feel warm shudders that rush down between my legs, making me so very hard. I reach for his cock, which makes my mouth water.

"Yeah, baby. That's it. Squeeze me."

"Make love to me, Nicco. Please." I open my nightstand drawer, bringing out lube and condoms. I stare into his handsome face, gorgeous eyes, and sinful mouth. "I want to feel you inside me."

"You will." He tears open the foil package and rolls a condom down his cock. "And so much more." He continues licking down my body.

When he rakes his tongue up and down my shaft, I feel my cock stretch and thicken even more. "Damn, that's so good."

Slowly and wickedly, he licks the tip of my cock, spearing the slit with this tongue. I close my eyes and fist the sheets, relishing every sensation he's giving me. I feel his hands on my ass as he swallows my dick.

"Oh, God. Yes. Yes."

My breathing gets shaky as he continues sucking my dick and fingering me. My heart skips a beat when I hear him pop open the bottle of lube. The oral pleasure never stops, as he slicks up my ass to take his cock.

It takes every bit of willpower to keep from going over the edge. "I don't want to come until you're inside me."

His skillful mouth releases my cock. "Then I best get to it."

He grabs my ankles and spreads my legs wide. I shift my hips to get into the perfect position to take his cock. I reach down and slowly guiding the monster, inch by inch, into my body. Once I have all of him inside me, the sting softens quickly, transforming into the most powerful ache of desire I've ever felt.

Holding firmly onto my ankles, he thrusts into me. It's so intense and overwhelming. I push into him, wanting more. I grab my cock, mad with need, and begin pumping furiously.

He slams into me, again and again. Over and over. Deeper and deeper. Stretching not just my body, but also everything I am. He's claimed me and I've claimed him. I'm his and he's mine. We belong together.

"God. Yes. Yes. Fuck." My words fall from my quivering lips hard and fast.

"That's it, baby. Take all of me." His thrusts keep coming like there's no tomorrow. "Come for me."

"Not until you come," I tell him, though I'm not sure I can hold back much longer.

"A challenge?" Nicco grins. "I like challenges. Let's see who comes first then."

The harder he fucks me, the faster I fist my cock.

When I reach up and pinch one of his nipples, I'm rewarded with a forceful moan.

"Playing dirty?" His smile drives me wild. "Fair is fair."

He shoves my legs even wider and begins pounding me like a beast.

"Fuuuck. You… win…" I surrender to his pleasure as my cream lands on my chest and face. Sheer ecstasy.

A second later, Nicco shoves his monstrous cock deep inside me.

I let go of my cock and pinch both of his nipples.

He closes his eyes and freezes, as if he were a statue. "Ohhhh! Damn, that's the spot."

Letting go of my ankles, he collapses on top of me. I wrap my arms and legs around him.

Neither of us says anything for several breathy moments.

I realize I've found the man I've been searching for my whole life. "I love you, Nicco."

"I love you, too."

Chapter 15

B*aby Malone*

I GLANCE BACK at the douchebag who's following me like a scared little puppy up to the prison gate. "Relax, Jaz. Everything is going as planned."

"Right. Whatever you say. It's just weird being in this uniform, about to go into this place."

"Just don't fuck up."

"Okay."

We walk up to the guard shack and hold up the counterfeit badges to the man on duty. With his ugly nose buried in a magazine, he doesn't notice us.

"Come on, buddy. We don't want to clock in late." This operation is time sensitive. Every second counts.

"Yeah. Yeah." He barely glances our direction before hitting the button that unlocks the gate.

Step one. Done.

On to step two.

DoucheBag and I walk through more gates. The guards who got thick stacks of cash early today look the other way, while the ones who are too foolish to get a payday seem oblivious to us. No wonder. This is a big prison. Guards come and go all the time.

Step two. We enter the laundry room.

One of the inmates tosses maintenance men uniforms to us. "Hey, Malone. You're a minute late. Teddy's hearing is almost over."

"Don't fucking worry about it, asshole. You just take care of your end."

"Sure. Done. Everyone is ready."

"Good." I look at Jaz. "Come on, kid. Time to earn the big bucks."

Step three.

I stuff my Glock into the pocket of the uniform and DoucheBag and I push a laundry bin out the door. We move a little faster than I'd like to. I don't want to attract attention but Laundry Asshole was right. We have to make up the minute we lost at the gate.

Just as we round the corner of a hallway, we're back on the plan's schedule.

Step four.

The door to the parole hearing room opens. A lone guard and Teddy, who is in handcuffs, come out.

Alarms start to blare. The riot has begun.

"Let's get on with it," Teddy barks at me.

What an asshole, but I have a job to do. So I smile. "Whatever you say, boss."

The guard, also on Teddy's payroll, looks at me. "You have to make it look legit, okay?"

"You're up, kid. I'm not busting my knuckles on this prick."

DoucheBag punches the guard in the face several times. The guy falls to the ground, his face looking like hamburger.

Using the guard's key, I remove Teddy's handcuffs. "Hop in, boss. Revenge awaits."

He smiles. "Texas, here we come."

He dives into the laundry cart. I cover the bastard with dirty clothes. *Very appropriate.*

On to the remaining steps—five through ten.

That will get us to Dallas and my *real* payday.

 *icco*

JOSH and I step out of the shower and begin drying each other off. I love touching his naked body, love everything about him. This feels so right, being with him.

Still, I'm worried. I know the kind of people who are looking for Josh. They'll stop at nothing until they find him.

I look into his eyes. "I'm so glad you finally opened up to me about your past."

"I'm glad too." He smiles. "It's like a huge weight has been lifted off my shoulders. I feel great."

"But I still have concerns. I have a good idea why Grayson wants you to move away. Your picture is plastered all over DFW in your promo ads for Red Shimmer."

"You're right, honey. That's why he's been pushing for me to move to Alaska. The band has become so popular, he's afraid the Southside mob will find me."

"He has a point. If anything happened to you, I don't know what I would do."

"Nothing is going to happen to me or you, Nicco." He kisses me lightly. "It's all taken care of. I made my point with Grayson. Just don't be surprised if you see some men you don't recognize hanging around. They'll be marshals."

"I'm not sure about this, sweetheart. I could go with you to Alaska. We could make a fresh start together."

"God, you are the sweetest man alive, but I would never ask you to do that. Plus, you don't know what that means. I do. It's an impossible decision. Go into WITSEC and you lose your old life. All of it. Everything."

"But I do get it. If you stay, you risk losing your life."

"It's going to be okay. I've been in Dallas for years and no one from my past knows I'm here. I'm safe. Believe me. Plus, Grayson will handle it. He's really quite capable at his job." Josh grabs his toothbrush. "I'm sorry, honey, but we don't have time to talk about that now. We need to hurry or we're going to be late to the wake."

"Okay, as long as you promise we can pick this up when we get back."

"Sure, baby. I understand your concerns. We will talk it about later, but just know I've already made up my mind."

JOSH and I walk into Mrs. Clark's home. In the entry is a large portrait of our dear friend next to an antique table with a guest book and a vase full of red roses.

"The flowers are a nice touch." Josh signs the guest book. "I'm sure she would have loved them."

"I know for a fact that red roses were her favorite. She told me so herself. I'll never forget how touched she was when Tony, Stephen, and I gave some to her on her birthday."

I sign the guest book and then we walk past the large spiral staircase.

"I had no idea Mrs. Clark had such a magnificent home," Josh says to me as we walk to the living room, where most of the people are mingling. "It's hard to believe that she lived in this massive place alone."

I nod, glancing at every person in the home for any sign they might not belong.

All of the people of Mockingbird Place are here as well as the members of the Episcopal Church of the Beloved Disciple. So far I've seen no one suspicious or out of place. But I'm going to keep scanning.

Until I get a chance to finish my talk with Josh, I'm his body-guard. Period. And as soon as possible I will meet with Grayson to get a better picture of what Josh is facing.

Martha walks up to us. "So glad to see you both…together."

"Good to see you, too," he says. "This is quite the party you and Sarah put together to remember Mrs. Clark."

"Julia deserves so much more, but we did our best." She wipes her eyes with a tissue. "Chad and Franki are in the backyard setting up your equipment."

He nods. "I better go help them."

"I'll go with you," I say.

"We got this, honey." He kisses me and heads out the backdoor.

Martha's eyes widen and she turns to me. "Honey? So you are a couple now. I can't wait to tell S."

"Be my guest." I hug her and quickly rush after Josh to continue my bodyguard duties.

Mrs. Clark's backyard is bathed in a warm glow from the land-scape lighting. The manicured gardens are impeccable enough for an English manor. The moon reflects off the still surface of her pool. The last time I was here the pool was far from still, being filled with the children of the church at a party hosted by Mrs. Clark. I'm still amazed at how much she was able to do for her church, for the community, and for us at Mockingbird Place. At any age, I don't know a more impressive woman.

Josh, Chad, and Franki, who will be performing soon for the wake, are nearly finished setting up. Around them are more people than were inside, but I recognize them all, which puts me at ease. No US Marshals. No gang members.

Josh straps on his bass. Franki moves to the keyboard.

Carrying his guitar, Chad walks up to the microphone. "Hello and welcome. Tonight we honor someone very near and dear to all our hearts—Mrs. Julia Lynn Clark. As most of you know, she planned out every detail, including the songs she wanted our band to play. This will be a mix of hymns, from traditional to old-time gospel music, as well as some of her favorites of our songs. Please feel free to sing along. This is the first song on her playlist for tonight. In her own words, 'Start with this one so that you can really get the party going.'"

Everyone gathers in close as the band starts off with an up-tempo melody.

The trio harmonizes, "When we all get to heaven, what a day of rejoicing that will be..."

Many in the crowd join in.

Father Stephen walks up next to me. "What do you think so far, Nicco?"

"She would have loved this. Look at everybody clapping their hands."

"She always liked the old-time hymns, and you and I both know how much she liked parties."

I can't keep my eyes off of Josh. What a sexy, talented man. How could I be so lucky?

As his band starts another hymn about the love of God, I turn to Stephen. "Where's my brother?"

"Inside with S & M, holding down the fort and greeting late arrivals." He smiles. "Is it true about what Martha told us? You and Josh are together now?"

"Yes, we are. It's very new and wonderful."

He puts his arm around me. "I'm so glad for you both. But be forewarned, your brother and S & M are hoping for a June wedding."

I laugh. "That sounds like S & M, but Tony? He has really turned into a romantic."

"Oh, yeah he has, and I love it."

"My brother is so happy since you two got together. He must want everyone to have the same wonderful life you two have."

"Same for me, Nicco. I really am happy for you and Josh. I think you two are perfect for one another."

"I think so too." I turn my attention to the man of my dreams as the song ends.

Josh smiles. "This next song may seem odd for tonight, but if you've ever seen Mrs. Clark dance, you would understand why it was one of her favorites. This is 'On the Run.'"

As he begins singing the upbeat song, I recall the last time I listened to it. I was in my car speeding to the tempo when Officer Mike pulled me over. I didn't know about Josh's past then, but I knew something was wrong. Now I know the truth. Josh is in real trouble.

When I start scanning the crowd again, which has grown since Red Shimmer took the stage, I see someone who doesn't belong here. It's Grayson.

"Do you know that man?" Stephen asks.

"Yes, I do." How I would love to let him know Josh's secret. I could really use his advice right now. But it's not mine to share. "He's...a...an acquaintance of Josh's."

"An acquaintance? Why would he come to Mrs. Clark's wake? Did he know her too?"

Unable to answer, I say, "Excuse me, Father. I'm going to say hello to him."

JOSH

WHEN I START SINGING the second verse of "On the Run," I spot Grayson standing next to Mrs. Clark's pool. Then I see Nicco marching over to him.

Damn it. I need to finish this song and get over there.

Chad and Franki join me on the chorus. "Don't try to follow me, I'm going too fast. Too fast. Too fast. This is my journey and nothing lasts. Nothing lasts."

But it's not true. It has to last. I love you, Nicco. We can do this. We must do this.

I know he needs more answers, but I can't let Grayson fill his ears with reasons why I can't stay. It may be difficult, but I know Grayson can make this happen for us. *He must.*

Nicco

"HELLO, MR. MANTONVANI." Grayson holds a cigar to his mouth.

"I have some questions for you, *Marshal* Grayson."

"Damn it." He narrows his eyes and in a low tone he asks, "What else did Josh tell you?"

"Everything. What I want to know is what you're doing to keep him safe."

Grayson looks at Josh on the stage and then back at me. "You're a smart guy, Mantonvani. If you know everything Josh knows and you care about him, then you need to help me talk some sense into his thick skull. I can't keep him safe in Dallas. Not anymore."

"He thinks otherwise."

"I know he does. Let's move over here so we can talk privately." He walks to a corner of the yard, away from the crowd.

I follow him, knowing how important it is to keep Josh's situation secret. My opinion of Grayson is changing. "Josh believes you are capable of protecting him here."

"I wish I could." Grayson shakes his head and places his unlit cigar inside his jacket, which allows me a quick peek at his pistol. "Ever since you moved in with Josh, he's been different...in a good way. He's never stood up to me like he did today. You gave him hope. I'm grateful for that more than you can know."

Grayson really cares about Josh. It's clear to me that he thinks of him more than just a person under his supervision. He treats Josh like a son taking on the role of a protective father.

"You've been good for him, despite my reservations, but I haven't had any bad reports on you except that incident with your old friend Digs at the diner."

"Digs is not my friend," I say emphatically.

"That's good to hear."

"So you had me followed."

"I sure did. I put a tail on you the day we met."

"That's good to hear, too." I repeat his words back to him. "I'm glad you're doing your job, Grayson. Josh is right. You are more than capable, even though you must now see you wasted taxpayers' money."

"I'm not so sure about that, Mantonvani. Digs took the time to look you up. Why?"

"He had a job he wanted me to help him with, but I made it clear that I wasn't interested."

"A job? Right," he says in a sarcastic tone. "So Josh told you who is after him?"

"Yeah, the man his testimony put away. Teddy Thompson, the former leader of Chicago's Southside mob. That's why I agree with you, Grayson. Josh needs to get out of here."

"You are smart. Like I said before, I'll need your help convincing him. You know anyone with Thompson's organization?"

"Not a soul, but I did hear about his reputation when I was in prison. You know about 'The Walking Dead?'"

"I've heard of it."

"That's what they call anyone who crosses him."

"That's a new one to me, but it fits. The bastard finds pleasure in making his enemies suffer before snuffing them out." Grayson sighs. "Teddy Thompson is why I'm here, Nicco. He escaped last night."

Chapter 17

J *osh*

I MOVE between Nicco and Grayson, trying to put distance between them. The looks on their faces are intense.

"You better not be trying to convince Nicco that I should go, because I'm staying," I say emphatically to Grayson. "We've had this conversation already."

As usual, Grayson brings out his signature cigar, clearly stalling because he doesn't know what to say.

Nicco places his hand on my shoulder. "Sweetheart, you have to go. We can't risk *our* lives."

I look into his eyes, realizing that Grayson has already gotten in his head. "He's wrong. I belong here with you. In Dallas. I'm not running again."

"We have to go. Teddy Thompson has escaped."

"What? No. That's not possible." I cling to Nicco because I

93

feel like the earth is about to swallow me whole. "All the things I've given up, the changes of names and places, the pain and the fear—it took over a year for me to be able to sleep more than a couple of hours without waking to every little noise, afraid that the beast might be breaking in to kill me or those I love. Everything I've gone through is now crashing into the present. The monster is loose. Is Thompson already hunting for me? I'm sure he is."

"Josh, I'm sorry but it's true," Grayson says.

"When did this happen?"

"Right after his parole hearing. Needless to say, they turned him down. Before the guards could get the bastard back to the main part of the prison, a riot broke out."

"Obviously all part of Thompson's plan." Nicco puts his arm around my shoulders and pulls me in close.

"In the confusion and with the help of two of his men posing as guards, Thompson was smuggled out in a laundry bin. A hidden camera captured what happened. Unfortunately, the video didn't get reviewed until the riot was quelled, nearly two hours later. By then, Thompson and his men were long gone."

My dream of staying in Dallas might be slipping away. I can't let that happen. I have to convince both Grayson and Nicco. *And myself.* "The FBI and every other law enforcement agency must be on his tail. I'm sure they will find him."

"Yes, we'll find Thompson," Grayson says. "But if you stay here, it may be too late for you."

The panic inside me is growing. More than most, I know what Teddy Thompson is capable of. But I won't give into my fear. "Just assign more men to my detail, like you did that first year after I testified. Twenty-four hour protection until the bastard is caught."

"I've already done that, Josh. Two of my men are parked outside on the street right now."

"You keep on impressing me, Grayson," Nicco says, turning to me. "But it's not enough, sweetheart. Not with Teddy Thompson. You know that."

His words convince me what I must do. *I will not put him at risk or anyone else. This is my fight alone.* "I hate it, honey, but you're right. I have to go."

"Yes, you have to go, but not alone. This time, I'm going with you."

"God, why do you always say the right thing? But I can't let you do that. It's too much to ask. You don't know what it means. You would never see any of our friends again. Never see your brother or mother. The price is way too high."

"Hold up, guys," Grayson says. "You don't need to argue about this because I can't do it anyway. This is a one-way ticket for you, Josh. I'm sorry, Mantonvani. It's just not possible."

"Make it possible," Nicco says in a firm tone that I've never heard before. It's clear he's determined to stay with me no matter what I say.

"Josh, is that what you want?" Grayson asks me.

Nicco leans forward before I can answer. "Let me worry about convincing him, not you. You just get things ready."

To my surprise, Grayson doesn't argue and puts his cigar away. "I'll do what I can, but I can't promise you anything. As soon as I know something, I'll give you a call. Until then, say nothing to anyone. Keep Josh out of sight in your apartment. My men will keep watch outside."

"Okay." Nicco hands his phone to Grayson. "This is my number. Call me when you have everything set up."

"I definitely will." Grayson puts Nicco's contact info into his phone.

They can discuss this all they want, but Nicco is not going. I love him too much to let him take the risk with me. This is the hardest thing I've ever had to do in my life, harder even than when I had to leave my grandparents and my sister. But how can I keep him from trying to follow? I'm not sure yet, but I have to do something. He may be willing to pay the price, but I can't let him. His family and friends mean too much to him. And he means too much to me.

Once I'm gone, he'll be safe. Me? My heart is already ripping apart, but that's how it has to be.

As Grayson gives Nicco's phone back to him, I spot Franki and

Chad motioning to me. "I've got to go right now to finish playing the songs Mrs. Clark requested, but no matter what you say, you're not going to Alaska."

Nicco grins, obviously not convinced. "Okay, sweetheart. Whatever you say. I'll be right here waiting when you finish."

"You bet you will, because we're not through with this discussion, Nicco." I turn around and walk to Chad and Franki.

Each step I take reminds me of what I'll be giving up. Now, unlike the other times, it crushes my very soul. How am I going to get through this last segment knowing I won't be playing with Red Shimmer ever again?

"You okay, Josh?" Chad asks me. "You look like you've seen a ghost."

In a way, he's right. Teddy Thompson has risen from the dead. "I have something I need to tell you and Franki, but it can wait until we finish the set."

"Why would you do that to us?" Franki asks. "You know how curious I am. This is an informal gathering so we can start a minute or two late. Can't you tell us now?"

"No. It's too important." I strap on my guitar and walk up to the microphone. "We have a few more songs Mrs. Clark requested we play. This is her favorite passage in the bible—the Twenty-third Psalm."

Franki is on the keyboards, which she's set to sound like a harp for the prelude. The crowd gathers in close, but the only person I see is Nicco.

Grayson walks away and Nicco moves in close.

As Chad, Franki, and I sing the song, one verse sticks out to me more than any other.

"Yea, though I walk in death's dark vale,
Yet will I fear no ill: For thou art with me."

I glance at S & M, who are wiping their eyes like so many. They know that this is our good-bye to Mrs. Clark. What they don't know is this is also my good-bye to them, to Dallas, to Red Shimmer, and the most heartbreaking of all is my good-bye to Nicco, the man who I love more than anything in the world.

It's difficult for me to hold it together, but somehow I keep my professionalism and find the strength to finish the set.

Martha walks over to Chad, who hands her a mike. "Thank you, Red Shimmer. I have no doubt that Julia is looking down from heaven right now and smiling. And thank all of you for coming. As you know, the funeral service is at ten a.m. tomorrow at the Episcopal Church of the Beloved Disciple, with the interment following. S and I will host a reception at Mockingbird Place at two p.m. that we invite all of you to attend. Father Stephen, would you mind closing out Julia's wake with a prayer?"

As Stephen leads us in prayer, my mind is swirling with so many thoughts and emotions. Where is Teddy Thompson now? How soon can Grayson get me out of here so that no one else will be hurt? What will Chad and Franki think about what I'm about to tell them? And how will I survive without Nicco in my life?

The collective "Amen" brings me back to reality and the here and now, which at present sucks big-time.

"So?" Chad is smiling, standing in front of me with Franki. "Is the big news you want to share about you and Nicco being together?"

"Chad, you need to let him tell us first," Franki scolds. "Not the other way around. So? Is that it? You and Nicco?"

Their excitement about what might have been steals my breath for a moment. I shake my head and clear my throat. "As much as I wish Nicco and I could be together, it's just not in the cards."

"Don't say that, Josh." Franki looks at me with her eyes full of concern. "It's obvious you love each other. You deserve happiness."

I remember saying those exact words to Grayson. "Even if it is true, it can't be."

"Stop being so negative, buddy. Franki is right. We've both seen how you look at Nicco and how he looks at you. Give it time. You're as right for him as I am for Blake, and he's as right for you as Blake is for me."

Realizing that I've let the conversation go off track, I say, "I didn't want to talk to you about Nicco and me. This is hard to say, but I have to quit the band. I'm moving away."

"You're what?" Chad's eyes widen with shock.

Franki shakes her head. "No way. You can't be serious."

"I know we're just getting the band off the ground. I'm sorry to leave you now, but I have no choice. I realize you don't know this, but Nicco is extremely talented and would easily replace me."

Chad says, "We can add him if you want to, but we're not going to replace you. Whatever this is really about, Josh, we're in this together."

"Yeah. Let us help you," Franki demands. "Talk to us."

"I appreciate the offer, but you can't help with this. No one can."

Chapter 18

*icco*

FROM THE LOOK on Chad and Franki's faces, it's obvious Josh must have told them that he's leaving Dallas and the band. It's clearly not what Grayson requested, that we keep quiet and tell no one.

Was Josh listening? Even if he was, I understand why he felt like he had to say good-bye to Chad and Franki.

It crushes me to know how difficult all of this is for him. If I could change it, I would. But Teddy Thompson has escaped and Grayson believes he's coming for Josh. We've got to get out of here. I'll never let him get his fucking hands on Josh. Ever.

My phone buzzes with a text from Grayson. *"I've briefed my men Miller and Davis about what we discussed. When are you and Josh leaving the wake?"*

"In an few minutes," I text back.

"Good. Miller and Davis are in a black Ford Taurus. They'll follow you back to the apartment."

"Thanks."

"Just keep him safe."

"I will." I'm surprised at my turnaround with Grayson.

At first I thought he was a total jerk, but now I know he was keeping Josh safe. *Is keeping Josh safe.* It's clear how much Grayson cares about him. I've picked up on their father-son vibe. No wonder Grayson was so forceful with me on the day we met. He didn't know me, and Josh hadn't told him I was moving in. I owe him for keeping Josh safe all these years.

While Chad and Josh continue talking, Franki leaves them and marches my direction. "Nicco, what do you know about this? About Josh moving?"

"I'm sorry, Franki. I can't tell you. Just know that Josh wouldn't do this if it weren't necessary. Please, don't tell anyone else about this. It's too important."

"You're scaring me. What in the hell is going on? When is he leaving us?"

"We don't know exactly when yet, but very soon. A day or two at most."

"*We're* leaving? Oh, so this about you?" Her tone sharpens like a knife, as Josh and Chad walk up beside her. "What have you done? Did some of your cronies from your past crawl out of their holes, looking for you?"

"Franki, stop it," Josh says. "This is about me, not Nicco."

"Oh, really?" She tilts her head slightly to the side. "Then tell me about his friend Digs that he threatened at the diner."

"How do you know about that?" I ask.

"Candi and I went there for coffee before we came here for the wake, and Lucy told us all about you and your friend Digs. So? Is that why Josh is ready to run off with you? You need to get away before your old gang shows up to collect on some debts you owe them?"

Josh moves between Franki and I. "I know you're upset because I sprung this on you without warning, but Nicco has nothing to do with this. I've already said too much, but know this, Franki. It is for the best of everyone."

"For everyone?" Chad asks. "What about you, Josh? Is it really for the best that you leave?"

"Like I said before, I have no choice." He sighs. "Please don't tell anyone else about this."

"This is nuts. I don't understand any of this." Franki's frustration is mirrored in Chad.

I can see in Josh's face that he's about to crack and tell them everything. I wish we could tell them more, but it's too dangerous.

I take his hand. "Sweetheart, we need to go now."

"Right." He wraps his arms around Franki and Chad. "I love you both so much." Before they can respond, he releases them. "Let's go, Nicco."

We walk out of the backyard and I glance over my shoulder at his bandmates. How many times has Josh had to do this?

As we pass Tony and Stephen, I realize I have to say good-bye to them too, but I don't want them to know it's forever. "See you two later."

They wave back at me as Josh and I walk out the front door.

I feel my eyes welling up as we pass Grayson's men in the black Ford. I turn my head so that Josh won't notice.

We get in my car and drive away. I can see Grayson's men following us in my rearview mirror.

Josh turns to me. "I heard what you said to Franki about going with me. It just can't be. You don't know what it really means."

I pull the car over and slam on the brakes. Grabbing his shoulders, I lock eyes with him. "I know exactly what it means. I spent ten years in prison. I know the price. For you I will gladly pay the cost. I love you, Josh. Wherever we have to go...Alaska or Timbuktu or some other place at the end of the world, as long as we have each other it will be okay. Trust me."

"I do trust you, but I simply can't let you give up everything for me." He breaks free of my gaze, turning away.

I touch his chin, and our eyes fix on each other once again. This time, his are welling up with tears. "Don't you think that should be my decision?"

"But—"

I place my finger on his lips. "I never thought I would find someone I wanted to spend the rest of my life with. But then you came along, the man of my dreams. Now, you're asking me to give up that dream. I won't do it."

He places his hand on my leg. "You're the man of my dreams, too, but this move won't be the last. Grayson will have to move me again and again now that Thompson is out. It's not the life anyone deserves." His voice shakes with emotion and pain. "Can't you see there's no chance of a real future with me?"

Knowing he needs the moment to lighten, I say, "I've always wanted to travel. And getting a new name every so often will add to the adventure. It'll be like we're superheroes."

He releases my leg. "You can't be serious."

"Oh, but I'm very serious, Josh. I would have no life without you. You are my life." I glance at him and then pull back onto the road. In my rearview mirror I see the Ford Taurus a half a block away also pull back onto the road, following us again. "As long as we're together, we can face anything."

"Damn, Nicco. You're very convincing." He smiles and squeezes my leg once again. "I just don't want anything to happen to you. There's no way of knowing if and when Teddy Thompson and his thugs might show up."

Chapter 19

T *eddy Thompson*

SPEEDING down a two-lane farm road in a motorhome, I look out the window. "Nothing but stupid fucking cows."

"We have to take the back roads until the heat is off of you, boss." Baby Malone, who is my trusted confidant, arranged my escape and secured this mode of transportation.

He had the motorhome's bedroom converted into an office, per my instructions. On the desk are several burner phones that I've used to call in favors from my old friends.

Clyde Walker, the moronic opportunist, thinks he'll be able to keep me from taking the Southside mob back. What a fool. Those men are loyal to me—*and only me*. Even from my prison cell I could have had Walker's throat slit at any time. But it was good to have someone minding my operation while I was locked up. I can't wait to see the look on his face when I get back to Chicago to give him the news of my return to the job. Then I'll slice the traitor's throat myself.

For now, I'm headed south on important business. All these years I thought the bastard whose testimony put me away was dead.

A light tap on the door makes me frown and has Baby gripping his gun. He's still jumpy after my escape, but I know we're home free. I had to move up the timeline of the operation after word came about the location of that scumbag, whose testimony put me away. Early or not, my plan went off without a single bump.

Baby shouldn't be jumpy. Still, it's good to see him watch my back. He's one man I can always count on.

Another tap.

"What is it now?" I yell through the door.

The door slowly opens and Jaz, the skinniest of the trio of idiots, appears.

"Sorry to bother you, but we have to stop for gas, boss."

"Where are we?"

"A small town in Oklahoma, three hours from Dallas. I know it's taking longer than expected, but we really need to avoid the major roads."

"I know that, you imbecile."

Jaz winces, which pleases me. Still, I owe him and his friends for finding that fucking musician. If it hadn't been for their buddy Digs in Dallas, I would have still thought the bastard was dead.

So, I soften my tone. "Besides, I'm in no hurry. I like to serve up my dish of revenge ice cold." I tighten my jaw, remembering the fucker who put me away. All those years he stole from me, gone. I will relish watching him die a very slow and painful death. "Find a place to stop where I can have a cheeseburger and fries. I'm starving. You have no idea what it's like to eat fucking prison food day in and day out."

"Yes, sir. I'll let Duke know." Jaz leaves and closes the door.

Baby turns to me. "That weasel has one of those voices that drives me crazy."

"Yes, he does, but we must tolerate him and his friends. I'll just keep dangling promises in front of them until we finish this job. Then you can take care of them."

Another tap on the door.

"Damn it. What is it this time?" I yell.

Jose, the fat one of the idiotic trio, opens the door with a cell-phone in his hand. "It's Digs, sir. With news about Josh White."

"Give me that damn phone." I take it from him and put it on speaker. "Digs, what's the news?"

"Josh just left the wake with Nicco, but there's a problem. It looks like there are two officers who are following them."

"Fucking US Marshals."

"Must be Grayson's men," Baby says.

I nod.

"And Nicco hasn't left his side since yesterday. That's three body-guards for Josh, boss."

"Digs, stick to the plan I gave you and Nicco won't be a prob-lem. I'll send you details on when and where to meet Pierce. He'll know what to do next. Let me worry about the other two men." I hang up the phone. "Damn it."

Baby holds up his gun. "Maybe you should consider changing tactics and taking out Josh right away. Our contacts in Dallas could set up something where I could get a sightline for a clean hit."

"No. I've waited too long for this. I'm taking him out. Get Pierce on the phone."

"You sure you want to call in that favor?"

"I know what you're thinking, and you're right. I only have so many chips left with Pierce, and what I'm going to ask him to do will use them all up. Still, it's worth having the best safecracker in Texas help me eliminate this Mantonvani problem."

"And since we know the little prick has a thing for Mantonvani, it will set the trap in motion perfectly."

"I just want to get my hands on that little fucker who screwed up my life and make him pay."

Chapter 20

J *osh*

NICCO PULLS into the parking spot next to my car and turns off the engine.

Before we open our car doors, he turns to me. "It's going to be okay, sweetheart."

"That's what you say, but I'm not so sure, even though you are very convincing. Can't I say anything that will change your mind about going with me to Alaska?"

He smiles. "Not a chance. I'm stubborn."

"I'm thrilled but I'm still very concerned about you. It's a big sacrifice with lots of unknowns. I'm glad I don't have to face this alone any longer, but I'm still worried about your safety."

He leans over and kisses me lightly, reassuring me. "We'll be okay."

My cell buzzes.

"It's Grayson." I put the call on speaker. "Nicco and I are here, Grayson. Any news on Thompson's whereabouts?"

"Nothing new yet, but don't give up hope."

I reach for Nicco's hand. "We won't." My real hope is they find the son of a bitch and put his ass back behind bars so we won't have to leave. "What about getting Nicco in the program?"

"Just got off the phone with the higher-ups." From his tone, it's easy for me to imagine Grayson chewing on his unlit cigar. "They're pushing back on taking Mantonvani."

I squeeze Nicco's hand. "They can push back all they want to, but I will not go unless he goes with me."

"Sounds like you're giving us an ultimatum, Josh."

Nicco grins and leans close to me. "You think?"

"Yes, I am giving you an ultimatum. I know that may be selfish after all you've done for me, but I can't bear losing him. He's my whole world, Grayson. He stays. I stay. He goes. I go. That's it. That's how it has to be."

"That's quite the turnaround, Josh, but I'm not surprised. I'd have to be a fool to miss how close you two have become. You've been on your own for so long. Too long. Mantonvani going with you is a good thing. If he'd been your boyfriend at the start of this, it would be a slam dunk for me. But I'm not giving up. I'll do whatever it takes. As soon as I know something concrete, I'll give you a call. Until then, I recommend you stay at your apartment. My men are there, right?"

"What men?"

"Nicco didn't tell you?"

"As you know, I had other things to talk about with him." Nicco points at the Ford Taurus parked in one of the visitors' spaces. "Miller and Davis are here, Grayson. We'll go inside and lock the doors."

After we end the call and get out of his car, I look over my shoulder at Grayson's men, who are also exiting their car.

I recognize Miller and Davis. Miller was on my original detail when I went into the program. Davis was the lead for Grayson's team when I was Kevin Curtis living in Oregon. Both are good men and very capable. I wave at them, glad that they are here, especially since Teddy Thompson is still out there.

We walk inside and I put down my guitar case. Nicco, as promised, locks the door. To my surprise, he also checks the other door and all the windows to make sure they are locked too.

"I'm going to check the upstairs," he says, clearly in protective mode.

"Okay. I'll open a bottle of wine for us. It will help us relax."

"Good idea. I'll be right back." He runs upstairs. A second later, he yells, "Should we start packing, Josh?"

"Not yet, honey. Let's just enjoy the wine for a few minutes." I grab a bottle of Malbec and two glasses.

Nicco returns. "Upstairs is secure."

"You do make me feel safe." I fill our glasses and hand one to him. "This makes me think about S & M."

He takes a sip. "Really. How?"

We sit down on the sofa next to each other.

"They were the ones who taught me to appreciate red wine. Before then, I mainly drank beer, and on the rare occasion I did drink wine it was always white and extremely sweet." I bring the glass to my lips, enjoying the rich, full flavor of the Malbec. "God, I'm going to miss them so much."

"Yes, sweetheart. We're going to miss them and everyone else. But let's try looking at this as an adventure. This is just the beginning of the rest of our lives together."

"I will try as always, honey, but I've been here for years. I've grown to love all these people so much. They're family to me." I sigh, thinking about Nicco's family. He'll be leaving Tony and their mother once again, and this time forever. His sacrifice overwhelms me. But what about their sacrifice? A sacrifice they aren't even aware of yet?

Images of my grandparents and sister float in the back of my mind and I feel my gut tighten. Jenny was only fifteen when I left and now she's a twenty-two-year-old woman. And how are Pappy and Grammy doing? Are they still in good health?

My phone rings. "Hello?" I answer, putting it on speaker.

"Josh, this is Miller. There are two men walking up to your door. Have Nicco look out and see if he recognizes them."

Nicco nods, moving to the window.

"He's doing it now," I tell Miller.

Nicco turns back to me. "It's Tony and Stephen."

"Miller, it's okay. They're friends."

"Got it."

"Than—"

The call ends abruptly, which doesn't surprise me. Clearly, Miller hasn't changed how he performs his duties. No-frills and always by the book.

Nicco opens the door and tells Tony and Stephen to come in.

"I know it's late," Tony says, "but Stephen and I wondered if you needed help with Mrs. Clark's eulogy."

"You might say that since I've only written two sentences."

Tony laughs. "Have you been procrastinating, brother?"

"No, just have had a lot on my mind." Nicco looks at me.

"Guys, if we all sit down and work together, I bet we can have this done in twenty minutes," Stephen says.

"I don't want to impose on you." Nicco's tone doesn't waiver one bit, but I know he's worried about them staying. "I'm sure you have your plate full with the funeral tomorrow."

"Everything is all set. Besides, I could use the distraction and the company." Stephen pauses. "Unless... we're imposing on you two guys. You two look so serious."

It's obvious to me that Stephen is sensing our dark mood, but I know that Nicco needs to spend as much time as he can with Tony before we leave. "Guys, have a seat at the table. I'll get two more wine glasses. Nicco, you get the paper and pens out of the desk."

The creation of Mrs. Clark's eulogy lifts Nicco's spirits and mine as we reminisce about her life. Being with Tony and Stephen allowed us to forget about having to leave this place, these people—*our lives*.

"Mrs. Clark would be so pleased with this," Stephen says with a grin, after our final reading of the finished product.

"Yes, she would." Tony finishes the last drop of wine in his glass.

"We better go, sweetheart. It's going to be time to get up before we even go to bed."

Stephen looks at the time on his phone. "It's already one in the morning. Time flies when you're with friends."

It breaks my heart when Tony hugs Nicco, and Nicco holds on tight, refusing to let go.

"You okay, brother?" Tony asks.

"Yeah. I'm good. Just tired, I guess," he says, though obviously I know the truth. But then he coughs a couple of times, and I wonder if he might be coming down with something.

After Tony and Stephen walk out and Nicco shuts the door, I look at him. "Are you okay?"

"It is difficult, but I'm fine." His heart is breaking right in front of me.

I hug him. "It's not too late to change your mind."

He squeezes me tight. "You know that's not happening. I've made my decision and it's final."

"Thank you for loving me that much." I lightly kiss his lips. "At least you can see everyone one more time."

"What do you mean?"

"At the funeral."

"No way. I'm not going and neither are you. Remember what Grayson said. We need to stay put until he calls."

I'm shocked. "So why did we write Mrs. Clark's eulogy? She requested you to give it."

"I wanted more time with my brother is why. Yes, she requested me, but I know she would understand. Until Grayson gets us out of here so that Teddy Thompson can't find you, I'm not leaving your side. And it's too dangerous for you to be out in public, even at Mrs. Clark's funeral."

"If we don't show, you know everyone will be worried and knocking on our door right after the service."

"I already thought of that. Tomorrow I'm going to send a text that we're both running fevers and won't be able to attend. I'll ask Tony to read the eulogy in my place."

"So that's why you coughed as he and Stephen were leaving." I grin. "Devious and stubborn."

"Exactly."

I look at him. "What do you think will happen once the service is over? They'll still show up at our door. S & M and likely everyone else will come with chicken soup and every other cold remedy known to man. When they see we're not sick, we'll be bombarded with questions that neither of us can answer."

"Maybe we'll be on a plane by then. If not, we'll deal with it as it comes."

"Listen to me, Mr. Mantonvani. You need to go to the service and give the eulogy."

"Why are you being so adamant about this, sweetheart?"

"Because I know what it means to leave those you love realizing you'll never see them again. I didn't get to say good-bye to my family after I witnessed the murder. I'm not allowed to contact them. It's too dangerous. God, I miss them so much."

"I know you do, but will it help to talk about them?"

I nod. "Remember me telling you that my parents were killed in a car wreck?"

"I remember."

"Well, there's more to it. I was five years old. How I survived the crash is a mystery. How my sister lived after being delivered a month early by the EMTs that very night is a miracle. All I remember is a loud bang and then seeing my parents lying on the ground. My grandparents on my mother's side took us into their home. They named my sister Jenny after my mother, Jennifer. As my sister grew older, she looked more and more like our mother. Although I was very sad about losing my parents, Pappy and Grammy showered Jenny and me with so much love it filled the emptiness in my heart." I close my eyes, fighting back the guilt inside me. "I never got to tell them what happened. After losing my mother and father and then me, I know it must have crushed them."

I feel Nicco's hands on my shoulders, causing me to open my eyes.

His eyes lock on mine. "None of this is your fault."

"I know that in my head, but my heart says otherwise. Nicco, you have to go to the funeral. Please, honey." I feel the tears rolling down my cheeks. "You can't imagine how many times I thought about breaking Grayson's protocol. At least hundreds, maybe thousands. I would hold my phone, about to dial their number just to hear their voices. But I always stopped myself because of how dangerous that would be. I wish I had been able to see my family just one more time. Please, for me. Just go."

"Sweetheart, okay. If it means that much to you, I'll go."

"You can't imagine how much that means to me. Thank you."

"But first, I need to know that Grayson and his men are going to make sure you're protected while I'm gone."

I bring out my phone. "Let's call him now."

Chapter 21

N *icco*

I GRAB my keys off the kitchen counter, still hesitant about leaving Josh.

"You look so handsome in that new suit." He straightens the tie. "I have good taste."

"You sure do."

Josh glances at the clock on the microwave. "You better go now or you'll be late."

"I wouldn't be going at all if Grayson hadn't assured me you would be safe."

"How you were able to get him to assign two more men to my detail?"

"Grayson and I have become close. Besides, I'm very convincing, remember?"

"Boy, do I remember." He kisses me. "Go and give the best

115

eulogy ever. Then hurry back. We have that afternoon flight to catch that Grayson set up for us."

"I'll sneak out between the funeral and the graveside service. No one will be the wiser. When they realize I'm gone, we'll already be in the air on our way to Anchorage."

As I walk out the door, I see Miller with one of the new men walking the perimeter of the complex. Earlier, I saw Davis and the other officer in the courtyard. I'm really surprised none of our neighbors have noticed Grayson's men, but with Mrs. Clark's passing they've had a lot on their minds.

I get in my car and drive out of the parking lot. This is the first time I've been apart from Josh since Mrs. Clark's wake when I learned that Teddy Thompson had escaped. Am I doing the right thing leaving? I'll only be gone an hour, and Grayson's men are very competent with their years of training and service. *He's going to be okay. I know it. But it isn't easy to leave him.*

Ten minutes later, I walk inside the foyer of the church.

"Hey, sweetie." My mom comes up to me. Right behind her is a man I don't recognize. "Where's Josh?"

"He's not feeling well, and he didn't want to make anyone else sick." I hate to lie, but it's unavoidable given the circumstances.

"Running a fever?"

"Uh. Low grade."

"I see why you care for him so much. Always thinking of others." She turns to the man. "Nicco, I want to introduce you to my boss, Kyle Paulson."

The man next to her extends his hand. "Hi, Nicco."

Despite my reservations about him and Mom, I shake his hand. "Hello, Mr. Paulson."

"Your mother has told me so much about you and your brother. She's very proud of you both."

"Did you know Mrs. Clark?"

"No, but I'm here to support your mother. She's very special to me."

"She is?" I'm not surprised. My mom wins the heart of everyone she meets.

"Oh, yes, she is."

"That's okay with you, isn't it?" Mom seems concerned.

"Of course it's okay with me, Mom. I'm thrilled for you." I wrap her in my arms. Knowing I won't see her again, I'm just glad she has someone in her life. "You better treat her right, Mr. Paulson, because she's special to me too."

"That's my plan, Nicco. I want to give her whatever her heart desires." He puts his arm around her.

"Kyle, you've already given me too much," Mom says shyly.

What a long way she's come. I'm so proud of her. Saying good-bye is so much harder than I imagined.

"I love you, Mom."

"I love you, too," she says just as Tony walks over to us.

He hands me the paper with the order of the service. "Your seat is next to Stephen's in the front. You'll follow Sarah, who will lead the first prayer."

"Got it." I look down at the program, trying to hold it together.

Tony is my brother. I've always felt like I'm supposed to protect him. But he doesn't need me anymore. He's a man and very capable of taking care of himself. And he has Stephen, who loves him so much. Tony will be fine.

"You having a little stage fright?" he asks me.

"No, just soaking it all in." I look at him. "The eulogy we all wrote is perfect for Mrs. Clark. She would be very proud." *I'm proud of you, Tony.*

God, I'll miss you and Mom.

I'm so thankful for the long talks Mom and I had. She felt so guilty about me going to prison, like it was all her fault. Even though part of it was, she was not herself back then. Not herself at all. Just looking at her now makes me so happy. I just got my mom back, if only for a little while.

And Tony? He's the best brother in the world. Even though it will be difficult for them when I disappear, at least they'll have each other.

As the organist begins another song, he says, "That's the cue that the service is about to start. You need to take your place, brother." He points at a side door. "That will lead you to the front. Mom, you, Mr. Paulson, and I will go through this other door to find our seats."

"I love you, Tony." I hug him and walk away, not giving him a chance to react.

A funeral is a terrible place to say your last good-byes.

I take my seat next to Stephen at the front of the church, which is filled to capacity, with people standing in the back. Mrs. Clark was beloved by so many.

As I scan the crowd and find Tony and Mom sitting with our friends and neighbors, I realize I'm not going to be with any of them ever again. My mind replays all the good things they have done for me. If it weren't for their collective help, I wouldn't have been exonerated and I would still be in prison. After ten years of being locked away, my freedom was certainly welcomed, but also a little daunting. But I didn't have to start my new life alone. Harvey loaned me a car. S & M got me in touch with the McBains, which led to me getting a job. Everyone at Mockingbird Place has welcomed me into their homes and their lives, including Mrs. Clark, who I will miss so much. I really hate doing this to them, just walking out with no word, no explanation. But it has to be. *For Josh's safety.*

Sarah sits in the chair next to mine. The next thing I notice is her nudging me.

I turn and whisper, "Yes?"

"It's time for the eulogy."

"Oh." I was so wrapped up in my own thoughts I didn't even realize she'd said the opening prayer.

I stand and place the pages that Tony, Stephen, Josh, and I wrote last night on the lectern. "I met Mrs. Clark the very first day I left prison. She brought me a bunch of her incredible homemade chocolate chip cookies. I can't tell you how great they tasted after living on prison food for ten years. I loved them so much and she never failed to bring me a dozen each and every week. But more than her tasty gifts, it was her love and wisdom she shared that meant so much to me. Julia Lynn Clark was born..." As I continue giving the details of the dear woman's life, my heart feels like it's going to stop. This is hard. So very hard. I have to clear my throat a couple of times to regain my composure. Thankfully, I make it through to the final paragraph without choking up. "I'm sure each of you have your own stories of Mrs. Clark that we can share with one another." *But I won't be here.* I point to the photo of Mrs. Clark that S & M brought for today's service. "We all loved this wonderful lady and will miss her dearly."

As I return to my seat between Sarah and Stephen, I notice something odd that makes the hair on the back of my neck stand up.

Four police officers enter from the back. I recognize Mike Tucker, the officer who pulled me over the other day. Are he and his buddies here to lead the procession to the cemetery for the burial service? Probably, but it seems strange to me they would come inside. I don't need to let my overactive, suspicious nature get the best of me.

Stephen leads the rest of the service beautifully. His words help to ease my anxiety.

After the final prayer, Sarah hugs Stephen and me. "Thank you both. It was a wonderful service."

"Niccolo Mantonvani?"

I turn and see Mike and the other three officers standing in front of us.

"Yes?"

"Turn around and put your hands behind your back," Officer Mike says. "I'm sorry, buddy, but you're under arrest."

Chapter 22

T*eddy Thompson*

I LOOK out the motorhome's window at the apartment complex across the street. My plan to smoke out the rat is working perfectly. Baby counted four marshals around the property. I'm not surprised. Grayson is no dummy. Still, the extra manpower isn't going to change the outcome. Mantonvani, the little fucker's lover, was just arrested. The bastard won't be able to sit still until Mantonvani is freed. Anytime now he should race out of his apartment to come to Mantonvani's rescue. When he does, my men and I will be ready to pounce.

"Everyone in position?" I ask.

Baby nods, patting his holstered gun. "Yes, boss. We're all set."

The wheels are in motion. Very soon I'll have my revenge.

Chapter 23

J *osh*

I FLIP through the channels on the television in the hopes that something will grab my attention, but no such luck. It's been over an hour since Nicco left. Mrs. Clark's funeral is likely over by now and he told me he was going to slip out before the burial service. I'm so anxious for him to get back.

Our suitcases are at the door, ready for the trip to the airport.

My phone rings.

"Josh, this is Tony. Nicco has been arrested for a burglary last night."

"What? That's impossible. He's been with me."

"That's what I thought. They're taking Nicco to Lew Sterrett. I heard you're not feeling well, but can you come down there so we can clear this up?"

"Of course," I say, realizing I have to talk to Grayson first. "I'll head that way."

"See you there."

With my heart pounding hard in my chest, I grab my keys and call Grayson. "I need your help. Nicco was arrested."

"I know. I just found out. McBain Charters, where Nicco works, was broken into last night."

"Then he couldn't have done it. He's was with me all night long."

"The safe was opened. He's the only one besides the owners who knew the combination. That's why he was arrested."

"We've got to get him out. Our flight is in two hours."

"I may not be able to spring him before your flight. But as soon as I can, I'll put him on the next plane to Anchorage."

"I'm not flying out of here without him, Grayson. Period. I'm going to the jail now to set the record straight."

"Josh, don't be foo—"

I end the call and race out the door. As I get in my car, I see Miller bring his phone to his ear. *That must be Grayson calling him.*

"Keep up with me, Miller!" I yell out the window before speeding out of the parking lot. In my rearview, I see him and his buddies jump into their cars and race after me. Good thing, since Teddy Thompson is still out there.

I turn left and see a motorhome that was parked across the street pull in behind me, blocking my view of Grayson's men. The fastest way to the jail is via Harry Hines, which has four lanes that will allow Miller and company to get around the motorhome.

The traffic light ahead turns yellow. Only my car and the motorhome get through before it turns red. My bodyguards had to stop because of the cross traffic. I don't slow down, knowing they'll follow as soon as they can.

As I take the next turn, the motorhome stays right behind me. Suddenly, a black Mustang shoots in front of my car, cutting me off at the next intersection. I turn the wheel and hit the brakes hard, forcing me onto the other street. I barely miss colliding with the idiot driver.

He jumps out of his car.

It's Digs.

What the hell?

Suddenly, someone else opens my car door.

The blood drains out of my face. "It's you."

Teddy Thompson holds a gun to my head and sneers. "Yes, it's me, asshole. Get the fuck out or I'll blow your damn head off right here."

Nicco

ONE OF THE detectives sits across from me in the tiny interrogation room. The other stands near the door.

The one in the chair is playing the "good cop" role. "Come on, Mantonvani. Make it easy on yourself. Tell us where the money is and you'll probably only get a slap on the wrist. Six months at the most. Maybe even just probation."

"Like I told you before, I was with my boyfriend all night long. He can vouch for me."

The one playing "bad cop" shakes his head. "Boyfriends are not credible witnesses."

"Then check with Marshal Grayson. You have called him, haven't you?"

"You're not running this show, asshole," Bad Cop shoots back. "We are. You knew the combination to the safe. You had keys to the place. It's cut and dry."

"If that were true, I'd already been locked up and awaiting trial. But all you have is circumstantial evidence, Detective. Either book me or let me go."

Good Cop grins. "Let's not get ahead of ourselves. We have more questions to get through to clear this up. I could use a cup of coffee. How about you?"

"I'm not answering any more questions. I want a lawyer."

Bad Cop glares at me. "Told you he wouldn't cooperate."

"Yes, you did." Good Cop stands. "Too bad."

The two men leave the room, locking the door behind them.

JOSH

THE CONSTANT RUMBLE of the motorhome suddenly ends. Since Thompson placed a hood over my head, I have no clue where he's taken me. I can only estimate the drive took around fifteen minutes. We must still be in Dallas.

His goons untie my ankles from the chair. Maybe when my legs are free, I can kick the hell out of them and make a run for it, even with my hands still tied up.

"I know what you're thinking, asshole. Do it. I dare you." Thompson's cruel voice and the feel of the barrel of his gun to my temple slices through my hope like a buzz saw.

Nicco

I WISH there was a clock in this room. They took my watch and phone, so I have to guess what time it is. No doubt, the flight to Anchorage will be boarding soon.

Damn it. I need to get out of here now, need to get to Josh.

I hear Grayson's voice.

"Open the damn door, Detective." He comes in. "Let's go. We're getting out of here."

I stand, anxious to leave. "How did you make this happen?"

"Miller and Davis's statements are your alibi. They knew you never left the apartment last night." He glances at the two detectives and then back at me. "Now let's go."

I follow him past Good Cop and Bad Cop. "What's wrong?"

Still walking, he says in a low tone, "We'll talk when we get outside."

JOSH

WITHOUT REMOVING THE HOOD, Thompson's thugs slam me down onto a metal chair.

One of them jerks my arms behind my back so hard it feels like they are about to pop out of their sockets. When I moan, I feel the butt of a gun hit the side of my head.

"Shut up, asshole."

I can taste blood on my lips and feel painful throbbing.

After they secure my arms and legs with duct tape to the chair, the hood comes off.

I blink several times as my surroundings slowly come into focus. It seems that this is an old abandoned warehouse, full of dust and debris.

To my left is the motorhome.

To my right, Digs takes money from a short, muscled guy wearing enough jewelry to buy a small island.

In front of me, Teddy Thompson stands next to a table filled with drills and other scary items clearly meant for torture. *My torture.*

Is there any chance of me getting out of this mess? Miller and Davis arrived too late at that intersection to know what happened to me. I'm certain that they are still searching, but how will they ever find me?

I would give anything just to hold Nicco one more time.

Nicco

. . .

GRAYSON and I get into his car.

"Are you taking me to the airport? We'll make it if we hurry."

"No." He drives away from the jail. "Josh was taken."

"Josh was taken?" Every muscle in my body seizes up. "What the hell, Grayson? You were supposed to be watching him."

"We were, but he took off after he learned you were arrested. My men followed but they got caught at a traffic light at a busy intersection. When they finally got through, they found his car abandoned at the next traffic light. It was only minutes he was out of their sight."

"Damn it." Guilt rushes in, crushing my very soul. "Thompson," I spit out his name like poison.

"Right. Two of my men reviewed the traffic cam video from that intersection. Thompson was there with his lieutenant, Baby Malone, as well as some people you know. Jaz, Duke, Jose, and Digs."

"What do those bastards have to do with Josh?"

"That's what we're still trying to figure out. We know that Jaz, Duke, and Jose skipped town and moved to Chicago after you were sent to prison. They've been part of the Southside mob ever since. Just low-level grunts. That is until now. We don't know what changed."

"And what about Digs? Is he still selling drugs here in Dallas?"

"Yes, he's been in and out of jail for robbery and possession."

"I think he's been following me since I got out of prison in his black Mustang. The asshole approached me the other day."

Grayson's eyes widen. "Are you serious?"

"Yeah. I thought it was about me, but it must have been about Josh."

"I bet you're right. Digs must have stayed in contact with Jaz, Duke, and Jose all these years. Somewhere along the way, they must have figured out who Josh was and used that info to get to Thompson." Grayson looks at me. "Wait a second. I bet Digs is the one who set you up."

"Maybe, but he's no safecracker."

"True, but Thompson has an associate that is. The guy's name is Pierce and lives right here in Dallas. I'll have my team pick him up."

"If a single hair on Josh's head is harmed, I'll rip his, Digs, Thompson, and everyone else's slimy hearts out and shove them down their fucking throats."

"Calm down, Nicco. There's an army out looking for Josh. We'll find him."

"I knew I shouldn't have gone to the funeral and left Josh alone."

Grayson's phone rings and he puts it on speaker. "Miller, what have you found?"

"The motorhome was rented in Chicago. The company equips all their vehicles with GPSs. We found it."

Thank God. Please let Josh be okay.

"I'm texting you the location now," Miller says.

"Have Shannon get a warrant for Gregory Pierce. Pierce is likely working with Thompson, and I have little doubt that he was the one who cracked the safe at McBain Charters."

"Will do."

Grayson looks at the text and hits the gas. "Nicco and I are five minutes away from the warehouse."

"We'll be right behind you, sir."

Grayson turns to me. "Open the glove box. There's a gun in there. You're gonna need it."

JOSH

MY EYES ARE SO SWOLLEN from Thompson's punches I can barely see. The connection between my mind and body is breaking. *I'm dying.*

"I enjoy watching you squirm." Teddy Thompson's words seem far away.

An image of Nicco burns hot in front of me.

· · ·

HE'S LYING in the bed naked and within reach. I touch his cheek. "Thank God, you're here."

"I'm here, sweetheart." He points to our bags by the door. "Alaska, here we come."

"Alaska?"

He smiles. "Yes. Where we'll be safe."

Suddenly, Nicco and I are standing on the top of the stairs of Club Midnight Hour just as Thompson and his men rush inside. Nicco and I bend down low.

"You shouldn't be here," I whisper, reaching in my pocket for my phone. Then I remember I left it downstairs.

I watch in horror as Thompson shoots the bartender three times. I reach for Nicco's hand, but he's gone.

When I turn back to the horror downstairs, I see that Alec is gone too. In his place, Nicco is being forced to his knees in front of Thompson.

"You've been holding back on me, McTavish, haven't you?"

I scream, "He's not McTavish! This is all wrong! Let him go!"

But no one seems to hear me.

"Teddy, I swear I've given you every cent." The words come from Nicco's lips but sound like Alec's.

"Don't bullshit me, asshole." Thompson places the barrel of his gun at Nicco's head.

I try to move so I can save him, but I'm frozen in place, paralyzed.

Nicco doesn't know about Thompson, doesn't know it's too late. I was wrong to bring him into my nightmare. "I'm so sorry."

Nicco frowns and his words sound like Thompson's. "It's too late for apologies."

"Boss, he's passing out again."

"Throw the water in the little fucker's face. I'm not through having fun yet." Bang!

I scream.

Nicco slumps to the floor, everything turns black.

THE ICE-COLD LIQUID brings me back to reality.

Thompson lifts my chin and leans in close. "You messed with

the wrong person, motherfucker."

The wind is knocked out of me when the bastard slams his fist into my gut. I don't care. Nicco isn't here, thank God. I'm no longer afraid to die. Nicco is safe.

"Are you fucking smiling?" Thompson slaps my face hard. "I'm done with this. You're time is up. Good-bye, asshole."

I hear him pull the hammer back on his gun.

icco

GRAYSON and I rush into the warehouse.

When I see Thompson holding a gun to Josh's head, I go into a homicidal rage. I don't pause to think. I just shoot the fucker.

Thompson drops to the floor as Jaz, Duke, and Jose fire at Grayson and me.

Grayson is shot and goes down.

With the overpowering need to protect Josh, I move forward and start firing at the bastards who kidnapped him and took ten years of my life. Each takes one of my bullets as they dive for cover.

Two steps away from Josh, I feel a gun pressed at my back.

"Drop your gun and don't move another inch."

"Okay." I bend down, placing the gun on the floor. As long as I can keep the focus on me, maybe he'll leave Josh alone.

"Turn around and face me, nice and slow."

I follow his instructions. The man wears a ton of gold chains and is a foot shorter than me.

"Nice work. You must be Niccolo Mantonvani."

"And you are?" I ask, wanting to keep him talking and his attention off of Josh.

"Baby Malone."

"I've heard of you."

"Good to know my reputation gets around." He glances at Thompson, whose glassy eyes stare out at nothing. "You took out my old boss, which was supposed to be my job."

"Your job?" And then everything becomes clear to me. "Clyde Walker hired you. The prison escape, coming to Dallas, kidnapping Josh. It was just a ruse until you found the right time and place to take out Thompson."

"Right. You're a lot smarter than poor old Teddy, and especially your three friends"

"They're not my friends," I tell him.

"Good, because they're not walking out of here alive. None of you are." He glances at Josh.

"Malone, don't be stupid. You don't have time to clean up this mess. You need to bolt now. There are more marshals who will be arriving any second."

"Thanks for the info." The hit man points his gun at my chest. "No hard feelings. Just business."

Bang!

A puzzled look crosses his face. Then he collapses to the floor, revealing Grayson standing behind him.

Holding his weapon that is still smoking from being fired, Grayson stumbles to the side, about to fall.

I leap forward and catch him. "I thought you were dead."

"Too mean to die," he says, his eyes closing.

I understand him, though he can barely talk.

Miller and the other men burst in.

"I'm okay, Nicco. Go to our boy."

I nod as Miller rushes to Grayson. Davis and the other marshals check on Thompson, Malone, and those three assholes who kidnapped Josh.

"Josh. Josh." His beautiful face is so swollen, bloodied, and bruised. "Sweetheart, it's me, Nicco."

I start removing the tape to free him from the metal chair. "Can you hear me?"

He doesn't respond. I check his pulse, which is erratic.

"Miller, Josh needs an ambulance!"

"Several are on the way," he answers.

I remove the last of the tape and pull Josh into my arms.

Chapter 25

N *icco*

BACK IN THE ER waiting room, I stare at the double doors that lead to where the EMTs took Josh a few minutes ago.

I dread the worst since he still hasn't regained consciousness.

Miller comes over with two cups of coffee, snapping me out of my thoughts. "It looks like it's going to be a long night, Mantonvani." He hands me a cup. "You'll need this."

"Thanks. What's the word on Grayson?"

"He's in surgery, but the prognosis is good. The bullet missed all his vital organs." He takes a sip of his coffee. "That guy you shot in the leg is also in surgery. The other two didn't make it, just like Thompson and Malone."

"Do I need to get a lawyer?"

He grins. "Not a chance. Grayson took care of everything before they whisked him off in the ambulance. You've been deputized. Any status on Josh?"

"I'm really worried, Miller. He hasn't woke up."

"Listen to me. I've been working with this kid for years. He's tough. I'm sure he'll pull through."

"At least I've got two doctor friends back there who will keep us informed."

Davis walks into the waiting room and sits down across from Miller and me. "Local PD picked up Pierce and Digs twenty minutes ago. Pierce was tight-lipped, but Digs sang like a bird. He confessed to the McBain Charter robbery and implicated Pierce as the safecracker. Now, tell me about Josh. How's he doing?"

As if on cue, Jaris comes through the double doors and walks over to us. "I know you're anxious to hear about Josh. The good news is his vitals are stable and his injuries aren't permanent. They will all heal in time."

"And the bad news?" Miller asks.

"Josh is in a coma."

I feel the blood drain from my face. "What can we do to wake him up?"

"Maddox and I have ordered a battery of tests, starting with an MRI scan. This will show us the severity of his concussion and how to proceed. It's very likely he will wake on his own." Jaris glances at Miller and Davis. "I've read the initial report, but there are a lot of unanswered questions, like who did this and why."

"We're not at liberty at this time to answer them, doctor," Miller says.

Jaris frowns, showing his frustration.

What he doesn't know is Miller likely has a ton of bureaucratic tape to go through before he can share Josh's whole story, even though Thompson is dead.

I can't stop thinking how broken and fragile Josh looked tied to that metal chair. "Doc, when can I see him?"

"I'll bring you back after his test. I'm sorry, Nicco. It's just a waiting game right now." Jaris goes back through the double doors.

"You okay, Mantonvani?" Miller asks.

I know if I say anything, I'm going to lose it, so I just shake my head.

The two marshals respect me and don't ask anything else. Miller steps away and makes a call. Davis picks up a magazine.

I stare into my empty cup of coffee. How can fate be so cruel? Why did I go to the funeral and leave Josh by himself?

Out of the corner of my eye I see Tony and Stephen rushing to me, which breaks the dam and the tears rush down my cheeks.

I stand.

Tony wraps his arms around me. "We came as fast as we could when Maddox called about Josh."

Like the tears, my words stream out of me. "This is my fault. I left him alone. I must have been out of my mind."

"I don't know what you're talking about, Nicco, but I know you. This can't be your fault," he says, as more of the Mockingbird Place family arrives, filling up the room.

Franki and Chad's faces are storming with worry.

"What happened, Nicco?" Franki's tone is full of panic.

Chad grabs my arm. "Who did this to Josh and why?"

More questions are fired at me, one after another.

S & M hold up their hands, which quiets everyone.

Martha says, "I know we're all upset and want answers, but let's give Nicco a moment to catch his breath."

I glance at Miller, who is still on the phone. What can I tell them?

Miller ends his call. "That was HQ, Mantonvani. We're clear."

I sigh and nod.

Sarah hands me a tissue. "Go ahead, sweetheart. Take your time. We're all here for Josh, you, and each other."

"Josh's story is long. Please be patient with me, but I have to start from the beginning. First of all, his real name isn't Josh White..."

When I finish telling them everything I know, the stunned look on their faces is no surprise to me.

"Grayson is the one who saved my life even after taking a bullet. He's been in charge of Josh's case since the beginning. I owe him."

"Where is Grayson?" Stephen asks. "I'd like to shake his hand."

"He's in surgery and the doctors say he'll be fine," Miller says. "We should hear something soon."

"And you are?" Chad asks.

I introduce Miller and Davis. "They've been protecting Josh."

"Oh, my God," Franki says, clinging to her wife Candi. "This is unbelievable."

"It's more like a movie than real life." Chad looks at Blake, his husband. "How did Josh keep this from us for so long? I've known him all these years."

"Honey, he didn't have a choice. He had to keep quiet."

I nod. "That's right. But not just for him, for all of us. He knew if anyone from Chicago found out about him, we would all be in danger."

"That poor boy." Martha wipes her eyes. "So brave."

"Nicco, what is Josh's real name?" Chad asks.

Miller steps forward. "I can answer that. He was born Leroy Brown, though his family called him Lee. Leroy or Josh or whatever you want to call him—he's a real hero. Without him, Teddy Thompson would have gotten away with murder and continued running the Southside mob. There's no way to know how many lives were saved because of Josh."

Davis nods. "He sacrificed everything for justice—never able to see his family or old friends again. It has been my honor to be part of his protective detail."

I listen intently with everyone else as Miller and Davis fill in more things about Josh's history. Pride for him swells inside me, as does an overwhelming dread. It can't end this way. I need him. *Please God. Don't take him away from me.*

Jaris walks back through the double doors and is instantly bombarded with questions.

Once again, S & M hold up their hands, quieting everyone.

"Josh is not in any danger," he tells us, "but has remained unconscious since his arrival. We've tried to wake him, but nothing is working. Nicco, come with me. We hope hearing your voice might do the trick."

I follow him through the double doors.

Once at Josh's room, I see him lying in the bed, with Maddox standing nearby checking the monitors.

I rush to Josh's side and take his hand. His eyes are closed. The wounds on his forehead and face are bandaged. There are so many wires he's hooked up to. There's an IV in the back of his hand, a blood pressure cuff on his arm, EKG leads on his chest, and more.

Seeing him this way crushes my heart. I look at Jaris and Maddox. "What am I supposed to do?"

"Just talk to him as if he were awake," Maddox says.

Jaris nods. "Let him know you're here and that everything is going to be okay."

I kiss his hand. "I'm here, sweetheart. Everything is going to be okay. I promise. Please wake up." I stare at his eyelids, willing them to open. But they don't. I lean in close, my lips to his ear. "You don't have to leave the band. Franki and Chad are so happy about that. Everyone is here. Tony and Stephen. S & M. Harvey and Nathan. Oliver and Adam." As I say each name aloud, I pray something will reach him. "Eli and Jackson. Trace, Luke, Ava, and Harrison. It looks like we're going to have a party once you wake up. Please wake up, sweetheart. Please, Josh. We don't have to run. We don't have to go to Alaska. We can stay at Mockingbird Place. We can start our life together. It's finally over. Thompson is dead. You're safe." I close my eyes, choking back the tears. "Please wake up. Please. Please. Please."

I feel a hand on my shoulder.

I turn and see Jaris.

"It's okay. You did great."

Suddenly, something pops in my mind. "Josh's family. Has anyone called them? They could help."

"I don't know anything about his family," Jaris says.

"That's right." I feel a sliver of hope rising up inside me. "You and Maddox were back here when I explained about Josh being in the witness protection program."

"He was?" Maddox and Jaris say in unison.

"Maybe Josh would recognize his family's voices. I'll be back." I run to the waiting room to ask Miller about Josh's family.

When I bolt through the double doors, I scan the crowd for Miller but can't find him or Davis.

"How is Josh?" Franki asks.

"Still asleep. No change. Do you know where the marshals are?"

"They just left. That guy Grayson got put in a room and they went to check on him."

"What room?" I ask anxiously.

"Why?" Chad asks.

"Isn't it obvious?" Sarah comes up beside me. "The man saved his life."

"That's true," I say, though the main reason I want to get to the room is to talk to Miller about contacting Josh's grandparents and sister.

Sarah takes my hand. "Grayson is in room 412. Go. We'll call you if we hear anything on Josh."

I rush out the door to the elevators. When the doors open, the sign says rooms 400-420 are to the right. I pass the nurses' station and find Grayson's room on the left side of the hall.

The door is open and I see Miller and Davis inside, with Grayson already sitting up in his bed.

"Come on in, Nicco," Grayson says. "These guys just told me about Josh. Did he wake up when you talked to him?"

I can hear the concern in his voice. "No. That's why I'm here. We need to contact his family. Maybe when he hears their voices he'll come out of the coma."

Grayson nods and turns to Davis. "Make it happen, but remember they've thought he's dead."

"Instead of a call, we'll have a marshal go over to their house."

"I'll get three plane tickets to Dallas expedited," Miller adds. "If they're able, we can have them here in a few hours."

Grayson smiles. "I always thought I would be the one to give them the news about their Lee someday. I would love to see their faces when they find out he's still alive."

"Thank you, Grayson. For everything. I'm glad you're doing so well."

"Like I said at the warehouse. I'm too mean to die."

I smile. "I want to get back Josh."

"Of course you do. Go to our boy. Take care of him."

Chapter 26

N*icco*

I RUSH through the double doors to get back to Josh's room. Jaris and Maddox are at the nurses' station talking with another doctor, a tall blonde woman with piercing blue eyes. She's so pretty she could be a model.

I walk inside the room and see that there's been no change. Josh is still unconscious.

I kiss his cheek. "Your family is coming, sweetheart. You'll be able to see them again."

He remains motionless, which troubles me. I was so hoping that when I mentioned his family it would reach him.

"Where are you, Josh?"

Jaris and Maddox enter with the other doctor.

"Nicco, this is Dr. Hakala," Jaris says. "She's a neurologist and specializes in traumatic brain injuries."

"Can you help him, Dr. Hakala?" I ask.

"I've reviewed his charts and gone over the tests. I'm confident Mr. White will regain consciousness, but I'm not certain when. It could be in a few minutes, hours, days, or even weeks. The best thing for you to do is to keep talking to him about his life. I understand he's in a band called Red Shimmer. Do you have any recordings of his music you could play?"

"Yes. I have all his songs on my phone."

"Great. The sooner you start playing them the better. In this kind of case, I've seen a variety of things from a baby's cry to a favorite television show that can trigger the patient awake. Sometimes they just wake up for no apparent reason at all. Just don't get frustrated. You have to keep trying until he wakes up."

"His family is coming," I tell her. "Josh hasn't seen them for years."

"That's good. It might do the trick. Try anything. Let him get a whiff of his favorite food or wine or aftershave. You see what I'm driving at?"

"Yes, doctor." I take Josh's hand. "I'll do anything to have him back again."

"I'll be monitoring his progress with Dr. Black and Dr. Butler. I'll be back later tonight to check on him, but if you need me sooner, Nicco, just let the on-call nurses know."

"Thank you, doctor."

As she walks out with Jaris and Maddox, I bring up my playlist of Red Shimmer. The first song on the list is "I'll Never Stop Loving You." I start it and place my phone next to Josh's ear. Nothing changes. His breathing stays the same. His eyes remain closed.

I switch to another song. "How about this one, sweetheart? I think you and Chad wrote this together."

The song ends with the same result. No change. *I'm not going to get frustrated. Doctor's orders.*

Stephen and Tony walk in.

"Oh, good. I need your help." I pull out my keys.

"Whatever you need," Tony says. "We're here for you both."

"Did you see the blonde doctor with Jaris and Maddox?"

"We did. Who is she?"

"Her name is Dr. Hakala and she's a neurologist who Jaris and Maddox brought in for Josh. She suggested we try using anything to trigger him awake. Stories, smells, music, just anything."

"Tell us what you need," Stephen says.

"There's a bottle of Malbec at our apartment that Josh loves. His aftershave is in the bathroom. What else?" I close my eyes, trying to think of everything. "He loves apple pie. Would you mind picking up a slice at Aunt Lucy's?"

"We'll bring a whole pie if it will help," Tony says. "And what do you need?"

"A change of clothes and my bathroom bag. I already packed it for Alaska.

Tony puts his arm around me. "I'm glad you both will be staying. It would have killed me if you had disappeared without a word, but I understand why. You love him."

"With all my heart, bro. With all my heart. But leaving was also to protect you and everyone else. Teddy Thompson was a very dangerous man." I turn to Stephen. "Before you go, would you mind saying a prayer for Josh?"

"That's why I'm here."

We bow our heads, and I keep hold of Josh's hand as Stephen asks for divine help for him.

When the prayer is over, I turn to them. "Could you ask Chad and Franki to come back here? Who knows? Maybe they can say something that will wake Josh up."

"Of course," Tony says. "By the way, I just got ahold of Mom. She and Mr. Paulson were at a recording session and weren't taking calls. When I finally got ahold of them, they left immediately. They'll be here shortly."

"I'm glad." Whatever hesitation I had for my mom dating again is gone. I realize now that all that matters between two people is love. The rest can be worked out along the way. And since Mom is clean, I know she's making good decisions now.

As Tony and Stephen leave the room, my phone buzzes. "Hello."

"Nicco, it's Gage. We just heard the news. I'm so sorry about everything. The police wouldn't listen to us. We told them there was absolutely no chance you were the one who robbed us."

"It's okay, Gage. I'm just glad they caught the guy. Did you get your money back?"

"We're supposed to go downtown and fill out some paperwork and then we'll get it all back. How is your friend?"

I look at Josh, praying his eyes will open. "He's more than just a friend, Gage."

"Oh. He's the one you told me about that you're in a relationship with. Is he okay?"

"He's in a coma, but the doctors believe he will recover fully."

"Listen, Nicco. Don't worry about work. Doug, Liza, and I already talked. We want you to have paid leave for as long as you need. It's the least we can do."

"Thank you, Gage. I really appreciate it."

"We appreciate you. If there's anything we can do for you, just let us know, okay?"

"I will." I put my phone away and touch Josh's chin. "I love you, sweetheart. I'm going to stay right here until you wake up."

THREE WEEKS LATER...

AT ONE IN THE MORNING, I check Josh's monitors for the hundredth time, though nothing has changed. "Sweetheart, your vitals are perfect, just like you." I kiss his cheek.

The items Tony and Stephen brought from our apartment and from Aunt Lucy's are sitting on the table. Nothing triggered him. No response whatsoever.

"Should I try them one more time?" *Don't get frustrated. Don't give up.* I grab his aftershave and bring it close to his nose. "Remember how you teased me about how good you smelled? Baby, I could inhale your essence anytime. Please wake up."

Nothing.

I remove the wine bottle's cork and place it under Josh's nose. "Remember that first night in the apartment when we shared a bottle of this delicious Malbec? God, I was already falling in love with you. Wake up and we can enjoy another glass."

Still nothing.

The same result with the apple pie, his pillow from home, the roses from Mockingbird Place's courtyard, and even the blueberry muffins Martha made, which I know he loves.

I take a deep, calming breath and look at the list that Chad and Franki gave me of Josh's favorite bands. "How about we listen to a Queen album next?"

Placing my phone on his pillow, I hit play.

When I sit down in the chair, I realize how exhausted I am. "Josh, I'm going to close my eyes for a bit and listen to the music, okay?" *I would give anything to hear him answer me.*

"Love of my life, you heard me…" I hum along to the song and slowly drift off.

"Lee is in here," Miller's voice jars me awake.

I open my eyes and watch him lead three people into the room. Retrieving my phone, I click off the song.

The resemblance of Josh and his family is quite clear. The silver-headed woman's eyes look so much like his, though tears are streaming from hers while his remain closed. The older man has Josh's nose and high cheekbones. The young woman looks exactly like him.

As the three of them rush to his bed, Miller steps silently next to me. We watch the long overdue reunion.

"Oh, my God, it is you." With tears still falling from her eyes, Josh's grandmother takes his hand. "My sweet, sweet boy. Your poor little face. It's Grammy, sweetheart. Jenny's here and so is Pappy." She leans down and kisses him on the forehead. "Please wake up."

I stare at Josh, praying for some sign of consciousness.

Nothing.

"Hey, big brother." His sister, who is also crying, takes his other hand. "It's me, Lee. Jenny. I can't believe this is you, but it is. God,

I'm so happy I don't know what to do. I just want you to wake up so we can talk like we used to."

Still nothing.

Jenny turns to her grandfather. "Pappy, you try."

"Okay, sweetheart." He puts his arm around his wife and leans close. "Hey, Lee. It's your pappy. Come on, son. Wake up. It's been so long. We didn't even know you were alive," he chokes out. "The marshal told us what you did. We're all so proud of you. We have so much catching up to do. Please wake up."

Josh still remains just as frozen as before.

I whisper to Miller, "I can't imagine what they're going through, what they're feeling."

"It's hard to say," he says, keeping his tone low. "They thought Josh was dead for years and now they find out he's alive but in a coma. It's a lot to deal with."

Josh's sister and grandparents continue trying to reach him but without any success. They haven't noticed me yet, not that it matters. I'd rather they keep trying.

Please wake up, Josh. We all want to talk to you.

Do they know he's gay? Josh left when he was so young. Maybe he hadn't come out to them yet. Whether they know or not, I doubt they have any idea that I'm his boyfriend. Do I tell them or not? They've already had quite the shock. What would Josh want me to do?

"I hear there's some lakes not far from Dallas that have some of the best fishing in the country," his grandfather says. "Sit up and let's plan a trip, son."

No response.

"Owen, it's not working." Josh's grandmother is clearly frustrated. "I don't know what else to do."

"I spoke with his doctor and she told me that sometimes coma patients wake up for no reason at all," I tell them. "We just have to keep trying."

The three of them turn to me.

"Oh, my goodness, you must be Nicco." She smiles and wraps me in her arms. "The marshal told us all about you."

I hug her back, wondering if Miller told them that I was Josh's boyfriend.

Josh's grandfather comes up beside us. "Son, are you okay?"

"I'm hanging in there, sir."

"Please call me Pappy." He smiles. "We owe you a debt of gratitude for saving Lee's life."

So that's what Miller told them.

"Pappy, don't be silly" Jenny kisses me on the cheek. "Of course he saved Lee's life. They're in love. Remember?"

"I'll never forget it, but Nicco is still a hero, right Marianne?"

"That's right," Grammy says. "And he's family too."

"I would have done anything for him." I can't look at them as the guilt rushes in. "But I left him alone. I went to a funeral when I should have stayed. This is my fault."

"Now you stop it, young man." Grammy takes both my hands. "Look at me."

I obey, looking into her eyes that remind me so much of Josh's.

"Miller told us about how determined Teddy Thompson was to kill my grandson. That's why Lee had to disappear and go into witness protection. He was so brave. It was horrible thinking we'd lost him, but now I know he was only trying to protect us. Teddy Thompson is the only one to blame for all of this. No one else, sweetheart, especially not you."

Chapter 27

J *osh*

MY THROAT FEELS SO DRY.

I open my eyes.

Where am I?

In a bed.

Where?

I look around the room, realizing this is a hospital.

Why am I in a hospital?

Seeing I'm hooked up to monitors and an IV only adds to my confusion.

Who is that good-looking man in the chair?

"Hello?" My voice sounds so weak. "Could I have some water, please?"

"Oh, my God, you're awake." The man jumps out of the chair and comes over to me. "Of course, sweetheart. I can't believe this nightmare is over." He takes hold of the pitcher and begins filling the glass.

I notice his hands are shaking.

He called me sweetheart. Are we a couple? I know I'm a man. Am I gay? Clearly I'm attracted to him. Yes, I'm gay.

He gives me the glass.

I take a long drink and my throat feels better. "Thank you."

"Josh, you're so welcome." He has such a nice smile.

Josh? Is that my name?

He leans down, clearly meaning to kiss me.

I hold up my hand. "I'm sorry, mister, but I don't know who you are."

His face tightens with obvious concern. "Josh? It's me. Nicco."

"I don't remember you... In fact...I don't remember who I am. What kind of medicine are they giving me? How did I end up here?"

"Let me get the nurse and have her page your doctors." The man hits the call button.

I take another sip of water, trying to recall anything. But whoever I am or was seems to be gone.

"May I help you?" the nurse's voice comes through the speaker.

"He's awake, ma'am. We need someone now."

"I'll be right there."

He turns to me. "She's on her way. Hang in there, sweetheart."

"I am." There it is again. *Sweetheart.* "What did you say your name was?"

"Nicco."

"And we're...we're...together?"

"Yes."

The nurse enters. "I've notified all his doctors. They'll be here shortly. It's nice to see you awake, Mr. White."

White. That's my last name. Josh White. "I'd like to sit up, if that's okay."

She smiles. "It's more than okay. Let me help you, but let's go nice and slow."

As the head of my bed begins to rise, I feel a little dizzy spell. "That's perfect. Thank you."

"You're very welcome."

"How long have I been asleep?"

"You've been in a coma for three weeks." She checks my pulse and smiles. "Your heartbeat is a little fast, but that's not unusual under the circumstances. Blood pressure is perfect."

Three doctors, a female and two males, come into the room.

"Hi, Josh," the female says. "You look good."

One of the other doctors smiles. "You picked the perfect day and time to wake up, buddy. All three of us were doing rounds."

"And you are?" I ask.

"He doesn't remember anything, Jaris." Nicco, my apparent boyfriend, is clearly very anxious. "Not even me."

"Oh, really? Then introductions are necessary." She's clearly not surprised at my memory loss. "I'm Dr. Hakala, your neurologist." She motions to the other two doctors.

"I'm Jaris Black. This is Maddox Butler."

"Jaris and I live next door to you and Nicco at Mockingbird Place."

Dr. Hakala places her stethoscope on my chest. "I need to ask you a few questions, Josh. Do you know what year it is?"

"It's...uh...I don't know."

"What city is this?"

I shake my head. "I'm sorry."

"Don't be sorry or worried. This isn't unusual for someone who suffered your type of injuries. I'm confident your memory will come back in time. You just have to be patient."

"What type of injuries? How much time?" I close my eyes, trying to will my past to return. But it doesn't. There's just this void. Black. Empty. "Are there some who never get their memories back?"

"Some, but that's very rare. You were hit in the head several times, causing you to have a concussion that sent you into a coma."

"Someone attacked me?"

"Yes," she says. "But this is a lot of information for you to take in all at once on your first day awake."

"How about a mirror? I'd like to know what I look like. Is that okay?"

The nurse moves the table that goes over the bed. She lifts the lid, revealing a mirror.

I take a long look at my reflection, which seems so foreign to me. I touch my face and run my hand through my hair. "I don't even recognize this person."

"You will in time, sweetheart." Nicco starts to take my hand but then stops.

"I'm sorry. This is just really strange. All of it." I glance at my wristband. "Even my name. Josh White."

"What about the name Leroy Brown?" Nicco asks. "Does that seem right to you?"

"Like the song?" I shake my head. "Who is he?"

"Well, it's actually the name you were born with, but that's another story."

"Maybe that's the place we need to start. I want to remember, or at least to know."

Nicco looks at Dr. Hakala. "Is that okay, given he just woke up?"

"As long as he doesn't get stressed." She looks at me. "The minute you start getting agitated, Josh, promise me you'll speak up."

"I promise."

"Okay. If you do, just rest for bit. Once you're relaxed then you can continue." She looks at the nurse. "As soon as possible, let's get him on his feet and see how far he can go down the hall."

"Yes, doctor."

Dr. Hakala turns to me. "We're going to leave you and Nicco for now, but we'll be back to check on you at dinner time."

"Thank you, doctor."

Dr. Hakala and the other two doctors leave the room.

The nurse straightens the bed and fluffs my pillow. "I'll be back shortly for your walk."

"I'll be ready."

She exits, leaving me alone with Nicco.

"Go ahead," I tell him. "Let me in on my life."

He pulls the chair close to the bed. "Let's start with where we live. This is Dallas, Texas."

"Dallas? That sounds so weird to me.

"Do you recognize the names of cities and states?"

"I do. Isn't that strange. I don't know who I am but I remember the United States of America. Dallas is in Texas, right?"

"Right."

"Do I have a Texas accent?"

"No, sweetheart." His face tightens. "I'm sorry. I shouldn't call you that until your memory comes back. I know it must sound odd to you."

"It does sound odd, but it must be difficult for you too. I'm sorry, but right now you're just a stranger."

He looks very sad. "Well, maybe if I keep telling you about your life, something will click inside you that will give you back your memory and you'll remember me."

"I hope so. Go on."

As he continues filling me in, I don't feel any stress. It's like I'm listening to someone else's story, not my own. Evidently, I witnessed a mobster murder someone in cold blood, which forced me into protective custody, never to see my sister and grandparents again. I lived a lot of places. Every move, my name changed. The last place is here. Dallas, Texas. The last name was Josh White, which everyone seems to be calling me.

"Oh, my God, Lee. You're awake." A young woman with an elderly couple rushes to the side of my bed.

"You must be my sister Jenny." I look at the elderly couple. "And you must be my grandparents. I'm sorry, but I don't remember any of you."

"Oh, honey," the older woman says, and then looks at Nicco. "What's going on?"

"He just woke up but he has amnesia. Dr. Hakala believes his memory will return. We just have to be patient."

Looking in all their eyes is so difficult for me. "I wish I could remember."

"You will," Jenny says. "You've just been through a lot."

I hate this. It's so awkward. Yes, they're strangers to me, but I don't want to hurt them. I start feeling anxious and out of control. There's nothing I can do or say to make them feel better.

The nurse walks in. "Oh. I see you have company. I'll come back."

"No. Please. Don't go. I really need to walk. Maybe that will help me to relax." I look at Nicco and the other three. "I hope you don't mind, but if don't get up and start moving I'm never going to get my strength back."

"Of course we don't mind, honey," the elderly woman says. "I'll go with you and the nurse."

I just need a minute to think. "No, that's not necessary. I'm sure I won't be gone long since this is the first time I've been out of bed."

The nurse helps me out of the bed. At first my legs are wobbly and my head is dizzy.

"Just take a moment, Mr. White," she tells me, keeping hold of my arm.

"I'm better now. Just had to get my bearings. Let's go."

Chapter 28

N *icco*

JOSH'S FAMILY and I watch him walk out the door with the nurse.

When he's out of earshot, Jenny starts to cry. "He's never going to remember us. It's like losing him all over again."

I put my arm around her. "Don't say that. He's alive and awake. That's all that matters right now. And just remember what I told you Dr. Hakala said. His memory will return. We just have to be patient."

I don't tell them everything she said, especially the part where there's a slight chance he'll never get his memory back. That would be too difficult for them. I haven't been able to get rid of this feeling of dread since Dr. Hakala said it. What if he never remembers me?

Shaking off the negative thoughts, I say, "Now we have to concentrate on giving him a chance to get acquainted with us. We're strangers to him. I'm sure he's overwhelmed with all of us showing him so much love. He doesn't know who we are. Just think how you might feel."

"I'm so glad my brother has you, Nicco." She hugs me. "You know just what to say."

"It's good advice, son," Pappy says.

"Patience is what we need." Grammy steps to the door. "Lee is already past the nurses' station, Owen."

"That boy of ours is strong."

She smiles and turns to me. "We'll get him back. You'll see. We just need a little more faith."

It seems that Grammy is sensing my fear that I may never get Josh back.

The overwhelming joy I felt when his eyes opened was completely knocked down when I realized he didn't know me. Night after night, I'd dreamed of our next embrace when he finally would wake up. We would say how much we loved each other. The kisses would never stop. But it didn't happen like that. He held up his hand and stopped me. How that cut me to the core.

But this isn't about me. This is about Josh.

I remember how disconnected I felt the day I got out of prison. Though I had my memory, I still had lost ten years and really didn't know my family. How much more unsettled Josh must feel right now. He's lost everything.

"Lee is coming back now." Grammy moves next to Pappy.

We all hold our breaths and stare at the door.

A moment later, Josh and his nurse Diana enter the room. I notice how hard he's breathing. Everything inside me wants to run and help him, but I don't move, knowing it would only make him uncomfortable.

As the nurse helps him back into bed, Tony and Stephen walk in. It will be obvious to Josh that Stephen is a priest since he's wearing his collar.

"Josh?" Tony's eyes light up. "You're awake."

"I am. And you are?"

Tony turns to me with a questioning look.

"He's fine, just a temporary issue with memory."

"Oh." He and Stephen move to the side of Josh's bed. "I'm Tony, Nicco's brother. And this is my husband, Stephen."

Josh looks at Stephen. "You're a priest."

"Yes, I am."

"Interesting. I guess same sex marriage is legal everywhere now?"

Stephen nods.

It's obvious Josh doesn't remember the recent past. What else is he missing?

He turns to his family and me. "Why don't you all go to the cafeteria? I'm sure there's a cafeteria here."

"There is," Jenny says.

"I thought so. Hospitals always have cafeterias. I'm glad I remembered that at least." He grins, which is the most wonderful sight I've seen in ages. "I may have lost my memory but I haven't lost my mind, right Nicco?"

"No you haven't. That's for sure." It's like he's the old Josh again, always trying to lighten up everyone when things get too serious. *I can't give up hope. I will get him back.*

"Anyway, I really am tired and would like to rest. So if you don't mind, could you please give me a couple of hours alone?"

"Sure, Josh," I say, realizing this is the first time I'll leave his side since he was brought in. I turn to his nurse. "Diana, you have my number if he needs any of us?"

"I do." Diana turns to Josh's family. "I have all your numbers. We'll take good care of him. Don't worry." She is our favorite of his nurses. She's been so sweet during all of this.

I let everyone say good-bye to Josh first, because the idea of leaving him is tough for me.

After they walk out, I step to the door and look back, hoping he'll say, "You don't have to go, Nicco."

But he doesn't.

JOSH

. . .

AS NICCO SHUTS the door behind him, I lean back on my pillow. "Maybe I shouldn't have sent them away. Was that cruel of me?"

The nurse pulls up the blanket and covers me. "No. You were absolutely right. You need your rest. This has been a very emotional time for you." She fixes the call button and places it next to my hand. "If you need me, don't hesitate to push this, okay?"

I notice the name on her badge. "Sure, Diana. That's a pretty name."

"Thank you, Josh. My parents named me after Princess Diana."

"She was a wonderful person. It's a shame how tragic she was killed." I frown. "Why do I remember that but can't remember anything about my own life?"

"I really can't answer that, but your doctors need to know this. It might give them information they can use to help you get your memory back."

"That would be great. I hope you're right." But deep down I'm afraid that black void in my mind will never go away.

Nicco

AS WE STEP up to the elevators, Pappy turns to me, "I'm going to take Marianne and Jenny to the apartment."

S & M and Oliver gave them the keys to a furnished unit at Cardinal Gardens.

"It was so kind of your friends to let us use an empty apartment at their other complex while we're here in Dallas," Grammy says. "I don't know of anyone who would be that generous."

"They are pretty wonderful." I remember how kind they were to me when I got out of prison.

"We'll be back in a couple of hours, son." Pappy shakes our hands.

"In that case, instead of the cafeteria, why don't we take you back to your apartment, Nicco?" Tony pushes the down button. "You need to get out of this hospital."

"That's a wonderful idea," Grammy says. "Get some fresh air, honey."

I hug her. "I'll see you shortly."

As the elevator doors open, Jenny looks at me. "I'm going to try to be patient, Nicco, like you told me."

"We can all do this together."

"But it isn't easy, is it?"

"No, it's not."

When we get to the main floor, I say to Josh's family "We'll see you later."

They walk toward the hospital parking garage.

Once I'm sure they are far enough away not to hear me, I turn to Tony and Stephen. "Thanks for the offer, but I can't leave. There's no way I could relax if I'm not here. I've got to be where I can run back to Josh's room if they call me."

"You're exhausted." Stephen says, "He's in good hands. All his vital signs are perfect, correct?"

"Yes, but—"

"You need a break, Nicco. Trust me. I've seen family members fall apart in these situations."

"I won't fall apart. Besides, what if his memory comes back and I'm not there? To be honest with you, I hate being away from him at all. It's driving me crazy that I can't be with him right now, even though I know that's what he wants."

"Yes. He probably just needs to sort out his thoughts."

"The cafeteria it is then." Tony leads us down the hallway. "When did you eat last, bro?"

"Yesterday, sometime. Five or six, I think. Mom and her new boyfriend brought me a burger."

"It's almost noon. You must be starving."

"Not really. I haven't had much of an appetite since this whole thing started. If it weren't for friends and family, I wouldn't be eating at all. I just never think about food."

"You have to." Stephen places his hand on my shoulder. "You don't need to be getting weak. Josh is going to need you, especially when you take him home."

Once in the cafeteria, we get trays and move down the line. Nothing looks good. I just can't stop thinking about Josh. But to satisfy Tony and Stephen, I make myself put some items on my tray.

"Chocolate pie? Nicco, that's your favorite." Tony grabs two slices, placing one on my tray and the other on his. "I thought hospital food was the worst, but everything looks delicious." He turns to Stephen. "Now I get why you like to do your hospital visits for your members during lunch."

As we take our seats at one of the tables, Stephen grins. "Well, since you're going to be working with me from now on, we could both have lunch here as often as you like."

"I'd love that, sweetheart."

It means a lot to me seeing how happy they are together. Will it be like that again with Josh and me?

My phone rings.

Chapter 29

N *icco*

"NICCO, this is Jaris. Could you come back to Josh's room?"

"Is he okay?"

"Yes. He's fine. Dr. Hakala has some things she want to discuss with you and Josh."

"I'll be right there." I put my phone away, telling Tony and Stephen what Jaris said.

"Go, brother." Tony points at the door. "We'll take care of your tray."

I rush out of the cafeteria.

Once back in Josh's room, I see him sitting in the chair with Jaris, Maddox, and Dr. Hakala surrounding him.

"Oh, good," Dr. Hakala says. "I'm glad you're here. We were just talking with Josh about dismissing him from the hospital."

"Isn't it too soon? He just woke up today."

"He's not in any danger, Nicco. There are two choices that I want to discuss with both of you." She turns to Josh. "I could release you to a rehab facility that would give you therapy or you could go home with Nicco. In my opinion, the rehab facility will not benefit you that much. It's just like being in the hospital. But if you go home, chances are something will trigger your memory. You'll remain under my care either way. If you choose to go home, I will schedule you at the rehab center as an outpatient if it's necessary. I'm thinking tomorrow morning for your release. That way you two can discuss it. How does that sound?"

Josh looks at me.

I nod. "That sounds like a good idea. What do you think?"

"I agree."

"Excellent," Dr. Hakala says. "We'll be here in the morning. No matter what you decide, I want to see you in my office in two weeks. If you elect to go home, Dr. Black and Dr. Butler have agreed to look in on you, if that's okay."

"If I choose to go to the apartment, I'm sure it will be fine."

"Good. We'll see you in the morning."

She, Jaris, and Maddox leave us.

"What are you leaning toward?" I take a seat in the chair next to him. "Rehab or home?"

"What a funny word. Home. I don't even know what it looks like. Tell me about it."

"I can do better than that. I have a couple pictures." I get out my phone and bring up the photos. "This is the courtyard."

"Very nice. I like the pool."

"Off to the left is our apartment, Unit G. We've only lived together a short time, but you've lived there for years.

He stares at my phone but clearly doesn't remember anything. "How many bedrooms?"

"Two bedrooms." I'm pretty sure why he asked that question.

"So…there's a bedroom for you and a bedroom for me?"

"If that's what you need. I want you to be comfortable when I get you back to the apartment."

"Thank you, Nicco, for understanding."

"I really believe that there has to be something at home that will trigger your memory."

He sighs, which tells me he's not so sure. "I guess I'll find out."

"That means you want to go home instead of the rehab facility."

"Yes. I'm hoping Dr. Hakala is right."

"So am I, swee—" I start coughing, trying to cover up my mistake. "Allergies, Josh. They're terrible this time of year."

He laughs. "It's okay, hon—" He mocks a cough. "I didn't know allergies were contagious."

I grin, wishing he would remember that he always called me honey.

Chapter 30

J*osh*

NICCO DRIVES us through a security gate. "This is it. This is where we live."

It's obvious he is looking for any sign that something is familiar to me. But nothing is.

"It's all very strange. I don't recognize anything. Sorry."

"There's nothing to be sorry about." He's been very kind to me, which I appreciate. "We'll take this one day at a time, moment by moment."

Every time he says "us" or "we," I feel my gut tighten. In my mind, I've only known him since yesterday.

Yesterday?

As hard as I've tried to break through that wall and enter my missing past, the result is always the same. Blackness. "Nicco, I'm not sure I made the right decision about coming here. I don't want to give you false hope."

"Don't worry about me. I'm fine."

"You're hardly fine. I realize this has to be tough on you."

"I can handle it. The only thing that matters to me is helping you through this." He parks and cuts the engine. "That's your Honda next to us."

"It's a nice car. An Accord, right?"

"Yes."

"2017?" The current year still feels wrong to me since I learned it from him last night.

He shakes his head. "2016. You got it last year."

"I see." As we get out of the car, I place my hand on the hood of the Honda. "I'm still processing that this isn't 2010."

Before Dr. Hakala released me this morning, she gave me a verbal test. When she asked me who the current president was I answered Barak Obama.

I'm still stunned that Donald Trump is the president. How did that happen?

Even though I can't recall my own past, it seems I have basic recall about the world. But that recall stops somewhere in 2010. Dr. Hakala speculates it has something to do with the murder I supposedly witnessed that same year.

As Nicco leads me through a gate, I ask, "When's my birthday?"

"March twenty-ninth. Next month. You'll be twenty-seven."

I look around the gated patio, which is quite nice but still seems foreign to me.

He unlocks the door. "After you."

I walk inside the apartment, praying I'll find the trigger Dr. Hakala believes is here. But once again, it seems I've hit a brick wall. It's so unfamiliar.

"It's a nice place." I scan the space. There's a small table and chairs near the kitchen area. In the living room, I see a brown leather sofa, several folding chairs stacked, a drum set, guitars, two keyboards, and speakers. "Don't you find it hard to navigate through all these musical instruments?"

"Not really. Besides, music is your life."

"Right. I'm apparently in a band." I pick up one of the guitars. "Can I play this thing?"

"Quite well, in fact."

"I wonder if I still can." This is the first thing that has had a sliver of familiarity to me.

"Why don't you try it out?"

"Yeah, I will." Praying my memory will be coaxed out of hiding, I strum a C chord.

Nicco smiles. "See. Go on."

"Okay. Here it goes." I close my eyes and start playing.

The music feels so good. So right. Every note seems to unlock the next, and the next. My anxiety about my lost memory begins to soften. Worry slips to the side. I'm consumed by a fast pulsing melody—a melody that seems to emanate from the void inside me.

And then without hesitation, I start to sing. *"On the run, never looking back, just moving forward. Don't try to follow me. I'm going too fast. I can't stop. On the run..."*

I keep playing and singing, sensing this song, its words, might be the trigger that will unlock my memory. Verse after verse sends shockwaves into the abyss beyond yesterday.

But when I finish the last note and open my eyes, I'm no closer to getting my memory back or knowing who I was before I woke up.

I turn to Nicco, with his eyes full of hope. "Sorry. It didn't work."

"But you remembered the song you wrote. It's a start."

"I don't think it is. In fact, I'm starting to doubt I'm ever going to remember." I put the guitar back in its stand. "I know that must be very difficult for you to accept, but it feels like the truth to me."

"Maybe it does now, but—"

"Wait. Please. Let me finish."

He takes a deep breath and then says, "Okay."

"You and I both know what Dr. Hakala said. Some people never get their memory back. I've been thinking about that since she told me."

"So have I."

169

"I realize now that this trip down memory lane has been a dead end. Nothing looks right about this place. I don't know why I was able to sing that song, but it didn't open up any new doors into my mind. I can play the guitar. I know the cities and states. I remember that hospitals have cafeterias, and a whole lot more. But that doesn't change the fact that I don't have any memory of who I am, much less the two of us."

His face darkens.

"We were a couple before. You want me to be that, Josh. But I'm not. I'm this Josh—the Josh who woke up yesterday. That's my real birthday."

"I think you're not giving it enough time, but let's just say you're right. So what if your memory doesn't come back? I love you, Josh. And hidden deep down inside, I know you still love me. I'm not going anywhere. We'll make new memories. We'll celebrate a new birthday, a new beginning. You fell in love with me before. I'll make you fall in love with me again. Trust me."

"That's just it, Nicco. How can I trust a stranger? Yes, I'm attracted to you. But I have so much to deal with. You said it yourself, we just moved in together. I know this might be hard, but you'll heal in time. Right now, I need to focus on figuring out how to navigate my life. I can't do that when ever time I look at you I see you grasping at straws. And when I don't remember something and disappointment in your eyes appears, I'm so frustrated."

"Don't be frustrated. You just woke up yesterday. We just need more time."

"There it is again. We. I don't feel that. I hate to admit that to you, but it's true. I shouldn't have come here. I'll stay the night, but I'm going to contact Dr. Hakala and tell her I want to go to the rehab facility tomorrow."

His stare is so intense I almost want to take back everything I just said. Nicco is clearly a good man. I can understand how anyone, even the old Josh, could fall for him. But I'm defective. Better to dash his hopes now than wait when it will be even harder for him to accept.

We stand there, locked to each other's eyes for several long moments.

I'm the first to break the silence. "Is this a battle of wills, Nicco?"

"No. It isn't." He steps right in front of me and grabs my shoulders, sending a quake through my body. "I listened to you. Now you listen to me."

Unable to resist his potent display, I nod.

"No matter how hard you try to push me away, I'm not going anywhere. Memory or no memory. You admitted you're attracted to me. That's something I can work with. It's a start. You see me as a stranger now, but that's going to change. Not your problem to worry about. It's mine. Yes, you have a lot to deal with. So do I. So does your family. This is how it's going to be. You're staying here. With me. *We* will figure out how to navigate your life. I love you, damn it. And if I have to love enough for both of us until I win your heart again, I will. Do you understand that?"

Fuck, this guy is impossible to resist. And hot as hell. "Yeah, I get it. The old Josh was lucky to have you. Maybe, in time, I can feel that too." I gaze into his gorgeous eyes. "If I do stay, it has to be on one condition."

"Name it."

"I know you're going to think I'm crazy after all I just said to you, but..."

"Well? What is it?"

I can't help myself. Something about this sexy stranger has awakened my body, if not my mind. "A kiss."

"You're serious?"

"Hey, it works in fairy tales."

He smiles, pulls me into his arms, and devours my lips.

My pulse pounds hot through my veins. It does feel like magic. My cock begins to stir.

He releases me. "Anything?"

"For me, that was my first kiss ever, and it blew my mind." As desire for him swells inside me, I trace his lips with my finger. "Perhaps rated-G fairy tales aren't quite strong enough for what I need."

He laughs, lifting me into his arms. "Okay, New Josh. We're going to skip through PG and R and go straight to triple-X and see if we can't unlock your memory."

"Yes. Please." More than any time since I opened my eyes in the hospital, I want to remember what it was like being with him.

He carries me up the stairs and into a bedroom. "This is your room. Mine is across the hall."

As he lowers me to the mattress, I pull his face to mine, thrusting my tongue into his mouth. I'm crazy about how he tastes. Delicious.

He strips me out of my clothes, tossing them to the floor. "You're so gorgeous, Josh. God, how I've missed you."

"You want some of this?" I squeeze my cock, pointing it at him. "Let me get a good look at your body, mister."

He smiles. "Memory or not, you're still a devil." He pulls off his T-shirt, revealing his incredible chest, solid biceps, and washboard abs. "You like?"

"Fuck, yeah. Don't stop. Take it all off."

He kicks off his shoes and does a slow striptease, slipping out of his jeans.

I can't seem to take my eyes off of his thick, hard dick. "Commando? I would have thought briefs."

"Depends on how I'm feeling, and right now, I'm feeling hungry for you." He licks the tip of my cock, causing me to gasp. When he squeezes my balls, I feel a lusty vibration from the bottom of my feet all the way up to the top of my head.

As he begins to lick my shaft in long, slow strokes, I fist the sheets. Watching him stroke his own cock while sucking on mine is so freaking hot. When his teeth rake the tip of my cock, I groan. Stranger or not, Nicco clearly knows my body's pleasure buttons, and he's hitting every one of them.

"Kiss me, Nicco."

He cradles my head in his hands and kisses me. As I feel his tongue caressing my lips, I part them, inviting him in. We both moan, capturing the other's breaths. With our naked bodies pressed together, our hard cocks sliding in sync, the friction pushes me to the very edge of losing control. And I love every second of it.

"Do I have a preference, Nicco?"

"A preference?"

"You know. Old Josh. Was he a bottom or top?"

"A little of both, actually." Nicco opens the nightstand drawer and brings out a bottle of lubricant and some condoms. "So do you want me to fuck you or you to fuck me?"

"Yes." I kiss him and then flip around on the bed, presenting my ass for his use. "But I'll take you first. Lube me up good, mister. I want to find out how much I like having you inside me."

"Oh, God. You're so fucking hot." He slaps my ass, and the sting he leaves feels wonderfully warm. "I'm going to make sure you like it."

"Triple-X, here we come," I say with a chuckle.

He starts caressing my ass, which makes me even harder. I feel his finger probe my hole, and my body tightens for a moment. I reach back and part my cheeks, slowly letting out a single long breath, which eases the initial resistance. He stretches me with another finger, and another, which drives me wild with intense, breathtaking sensations.

I glance over my shoulder and see that his cock is even harder. "Nicco, take my ass and let me see what it's like."

He kisses the small of my back and then gets on top of me. I feel the head of his cock pressing against my stretched and slicked up ring, which makes me moan in anticipation of more pleasure.

Then he slips the tip of his dick into me. The pressure is overwhelming, so much more than what his three fingers created. He captures my ear between his teeth and thrusts slowly, all the way into my ass. Once he's fully seated inside me, I shift my hips to push back into him, rubbing my cock against the sheets, the friction heightening my lust.

I can't control my moans. They just keep coming and coming, like from a wild animal. I can hear Nicco's groans getting louder, as his thrusts into my body come faster and faster, so hard they shake the bed. Every time he slams into me, it sends a quivering sensation down into my cock.

"I'm...close...Josh...so...very...close."

"Oh, yes. Yes. Yes." I thrust back and forth against him and the bed, desperate for us to come together.

A deep, primal groan leaves his lips, warming my neck with his hot breath. "Fuuuck!"

When I feel him come inside me, my cock pulses, shooting hot liquid onto the sheets. The sensations shooting through my body are staggering. It takes me several moments to catch my breath.

Nicco rolls off of me, and I get on my side, facing him.

Even his after-sex panting seems to flip a switch inside me as my cock already begins to stir again. I smile, wrap my hands around his neck, and draw him in for a kiss.

"Damn, Josh. I missed this so much, missed you."

"Just wait, mister. I'm not done. I'm going to make slow love to you." As I kiss his neck, I pinch his nipples.

"Oh, yeah, you are. Mm. That feels so good."

"On your stomach, sailor," I command.

He grins and gives me a mock salute. "Aye, aye, captain."

When he rolls over, the ass he presents is flawless, a bubble-butt masterpiece. My need to take him is so unrelenting, I waste no time lubing him up.

"I want to look in your eyes when I fuck you. On your back."

He flips around and I place a pillow under the small of his back to better position him for my cock. I slide my cock into him, and he traps my body by locking his ankles behind my back and grasping my shoulders with his hands.

I thrust into him with a steady rocking motion.

"Keep going, Josh. Don't stop. Give it to me."

I can feel him tightening his ass around my cock.

Suddenly, he flips us both around, placing my back on the bed and him on top of me. Even though it's his turn to bottom, he still remains dominant and in control. He rides me like a cowboy and I thrust into him as hard as I can. His movements are fierce—up and down, side to side, forward and back. I grab his thick cock as he presses on my nipples until they are throbbing like mad.

I explode inside him, surrendering completely to the pleasure he's given me.

A moment later, he groans, shooting his cream onto my chest and face. Then he tumbles on top of me, his weight securing me under him.

The vibrations in my body begin to subside slowly. We remain in each other's arms, my head on his shoulder.

Is this what it was like with him before? I don't remember, but I can't imagine sex being more passionate.

I listen to his heartbeat as we both start to slip off to sleep.

Chapter 31

N*icco*

THE NEXT MORNING I slip quietly out of bed, trying not to disturb Josh. He looks so content, eyes closed and sleeping soundly. *We didn't need two bedrooms after all.*

I walk out and gently close the door. I want to make a fantastic breakfast for him. Will he still like pancakes? I smile, thinking of last night. He definitely liked some of the same things in bed. It was just like before when he knew he was in love with me.

Once in the kitchen, I pull out the griddle and start the coffee.

Even if he doesn't regain his memory, we can still have a great life together. And I feel in my heart he will love me again. The spark we felt before is still there. I could tell by the way he looked at me, touched me. It was heaven on earth.

God, I love him so very much.

I hope I'm not kidding myself.

No, I can't be.

Maybe, just maybe he felt something more than sex.

If someone could read my mind right now, they would believe I've gone off the deep end, thinking this way, always in circles. Back and forth. Up and down. It's just too much to take in.

We'll get pass this. I know we will. *Or will we?*

Damn, here I go again.

I'll just cook breakfast and try not to think. I know what I'll do. I'll sing.

As I place the bacon in the frying pan, I start singing "You've Lost That Lovin' Feelin'."

That certainly didn't work. Guess there's no hope of getting this off my mind.

JOSH

WHEN I FEEL the warmth of the sun on my face, I open my eyes and sit up in the bed.

Where's Nicco?

I can still feel his arms around me. God, what a night. He's a sexual beast. At least the best lover I've ever had in my short two-day existence. *The only lover I've ever had.* I can't imagine anyone being any better than him. It was like our bodies and desires were perfectly matched.

I pull on my jeans and walk to the door. When I open it, I'm hit with the glorious smell of bacon, which makes my stomach rumble. "Nicco, are you cooking breakfast?"

"I am. Come on down. It's almost ready."

I bound down the stairs and find him standing at the stove. "Is that pancakes?"

He nods. "I was wondering if bacon and pancakes were still your favorite."

"I don't know, but it sure does smell good."

"Can you pour us some coffee?" Nicco is stacking golden brown pancakes on a platter.

I look around the kitchen. "Where are the cups?"

Nicco points at the upper cabinet next to the sink.

I leave one black and mix in cream and sugar in the other. "Unleaded for you," I say, handing him his cup. "And leaded for me."

He turns to me. "How did you remember that?"

"I don't know. It just seemed automatic." I take a sip. "I was right. It's delicious."

"Great. Everything is ready. Let's eat."

He places a big stack of pancakes with what looks to be a half a pound of crispy bacon in front of me.

"I'm not sure I can eat all of this, Nicco."

"After our workout last night, I'm sure you can."

"All I know is that last night was the most wonderful, exciting thing I've ever experienced." I take my first bite. "Mm. This is wonderful."

"I'm glad you like it."

"Life is fabulous, isn't it? I really didn't have any idea that sex was so good. Can we do it again?"

"Hold on, Josh. Yes, sex is wonderful, but it is even greater when you're in love. Do you remember the term making love? That's how I felt. I was making love to you. You were having sex with me. Do you understand what I'm saying?"

"Yes, I get it, but I really would enjoy the process again unless it hurts you that it is just sex for me." I can't help but smile. The experience was so overpowering.

Nicco grins and then starts laughing.

"What's so funny?" I ask. "Was I terrible?"

"Absolutely not. You were quite amazing…for a virgin." Then he starts laughing again.

"Oh, I get it. I'm not really a virgin but it's like my first time."

"Yes, and it really isn't funny." His tone turns serious. "It's just that for weeks now I've been so stressed. Then we have this amazing sex for you and making love for me. I just exploded with happiness. There are no words to explain how I feel, but I would enjoy *this process*, as you put it, one more time. You game?"

"Absolutely, I would like nothing better." I lean over and kiss him passionately. "Virgin, aye? Maybe I'll remember some tricks for next time."

"Next time?" He smiles. "I think next time is right now. Are you finished with your breakfast?"

"Yes, I'm finished."

"Good." Nicco stands and grabs up all our dishes in one swoop.

"I'm going to run upstairs and take a quick shower." I jump to my feet.

"Perfect. I think I'll join you."

"Better catch me first." I take off running.

Three steps later, I hear a loud crash behind me. "Nicco, get down!"

I WATCH in horror as Thompson shoots the bartender three times. I reach for Nicco's hand, but he's gone.

When I turn back to the horror downstairs, Nicco is being forced to his knees in front of Thompson.

I RUSH TO NICCO, knocking him down and covering his body with mine. "I won't let him kill you."

From the floor, Nicco grabs my shoulders. "Josh. Josh. Are you okay? There's no one here but us."

"Oh, my God, honey. I remember. I remember everything. I remember how much I love you." I shower him with kisses. "I love you so much."

"I love you, too, Josh," he says with tears streaming down his face.

"This is the best day of my life. I'm so happy."

"I'm happy too, sweetheart. But would you mind letting me up?" He smiles. "A fork is stabbing me in the back."

"Oh, I'm sorry." I stand and help him to his feet. Seeing the debris of our breakfast on the floor makes me I laugh. "You look so good in pancakes. I'm just so happy. Oh, my God. My family. I saw

them. I have to call them. Jenny is all grown up. I have to call everybody. How about a party?" I can't hold in my excitement. "I have
my life again. Let's not tell everyone I got my memory back. That
way we can make it a surprise party."

"Honey, take a breath." Smiling, he pulls me into his arms, and
we kiss.

"If we're going to have a party, sweetheart," he says, "I better
get this mess cleaned up while you invite everyone over."

I grab my phone and call my family first. Grammy made sure I
had her number before she left yesterday.

"Hello."

"Grammy, it's Lee. I remember everything. Please come over. I
need to hold you in my arms. You, Jenny, and Pappy. I can't wait to
see you."

"Honey, we are just next door in the other apartment complex.
Owen, Jenny, he's got his memory back. I know. I know. It's wonderful. Sweetheart, we'll be right there."

"I love you. Hurry."

"Nicco," I yell into the kitchen, putting my phone away. "I told
Grammy. When I heard her voice I just couldn't pretend with her.
They're on their way right now. I'm so excited."

"I hope they won't mind this mess. I've hardly begun to clean
it up."

"It will be fine, especially when we explain this mess was how I
got my memory back. In fact, let's just leave it for everyone to see.
It's a beautiful mess. I want a picture. Smile, honey."

He grins, holding up the broom.

I capture the moment with my phone. "I love it."

"Since you have a picture, I think I'll clean it before some ant
comes around thinking he's in heaven."

"Okay, if you insist."

"I insist. You enjoy your family and I'll finish this. Then I'll call
our friends and tell them we're having a welcome home party for
you. That way everyone else will be surprised."

"Honey, you're the greatest. Have I told you lately that I love
you?"

"Yes, but I will never tire of hearing it. I love you, too, so very much."

The doorbell rings.

"It's my family." I jump up so fast I nearly run into the coffee table. I open the door and am grabbed with three sets of arms. We hug, cry, and laugh all at the same time. It's beautiful.

Nicco takes my hand. "Invite them in, sweetheart. We don't want anyone else to see you and catch on that you've got your memory back. We still want to surprise everyone else, right?"

"You're right." I turn to my family. "Come on inside. Hurry."

They walk in and I shut the door.

"Jenny, you are beautiful. You look just like Mom. Sit down, everyone."

Nicco walks in carrying a tray with a fresh pot of coffee, cups, cream and sugar on it. "I would like to offer you more, but we haven't been to the store since we got home. And please forgive the mess in the kitchen. Josh can tell you about that."

"Coffee is perfect and I couldn't care less about a mess." Pappy gets a cup. "I'm just so happy we have our Lee back. How about you, Marianne. You want some coffee?"

"Yes, honey. Jenny?" Grammy asks.

"I would love one, but something tells me there's a good story about the debris in the kitchen."

I stand as if I'm on stage and tell them the whole story of how I got my memory back.

Jenny looks at me, "Have you told your doctors yet?"

"No, but——"

"Well you should do that right now."

"Gee, some things or some people never change," I tease.

"Well, don't you think you should be checked or get their opinion?"

"Jen, you don't have to worry, I feel utterly fantastic. Besides, I'm inviting them as well as everyone else to a welcome home party. I don't want anyone to know I've got my memory back. It will be a big surprise."

Nicco walks into the living room. "I finally got everything back in order, that is except me. I'm going to take a shower and then call S & M. I thought I'd ask them to call everyone about the party. Then I'll head to the store and get some things we'll need for tonight. That will give you all a chance to catch up."

"Thanks, honey. You're doing everything. I should help."

"No. I want you to have this time with your family. You need this and so do they."

"You see why I love him so much?"

"You might say we knew before you did." Grammy laughs. "After all, he saved your life."

"He what?" I turn to Nicco. "What does she mean? What happened after I passed out in the warehouse?"

He recounts everything that happened.

"Oh, my God, honey. You're a hero." I wrap my arms around him. "You're *my* hero."

Chapter 32

N *icco*

THE DOORBELL RINGS.

"Our first guests." Josh's eyes are full of glee. "You open the door. I'll do the rest."

"You're enjoying this surprise a little too much." I grin, looking out the peephole. "It's S & M and they're carrying tons of food. Please don't say anything until I get the dishes from them or the kitchen will be a mess again."

"Okay. Okay. I'll try. Look at me, honey. Do I have a sad face?"

"Yes. That's perfect." I open the door. "Come on in. Let me help you with that."

Before they hand me a single dish, Martha turns to Josh. "Are you okay, sweetheart? You look so upset."

A huge smile breaks out on his face. "I'm fine. Really fine. My memory is back. I really know who you are."

And just as I expected, S & M start an Irish jig, barely holding on to their dishes. Josh and I quickly grab the food and place it on the coffee table, avoiding another catastrophe.

"I'm sorry, honey," he says. "I just couldn't hold it in."

"Don't you dare hold good news like that from us ever again." Martha pulls him into her arms.

Sarah wraps her arms around all of us. "When did this happen?"

Before Josh or I could answer, the doorbell rings.

I look out the peephole. "It's Tony and Stephen. They have food too."

"Let's all sit down like we're very sad," Martha says, clearly wanting to get in on the surprise.

"Yes. Yes." Josh looks at me. "I'll be quiet this time until you get the food set down."

I grin. "I don't believe you. Sad faces everyone. Perfect."

I open the door.

Tony and Stephen glance at the gloomy-looking trio on the sofa.

Tony turns to me. "What's the bad news?"

"Do I need to pray?" Stephen asks.

Martha bursts out laughing and Sarah yells, "Surprise!"

"Surprise?" Tony and Stephen say together.

"I didn't do it this time, Nicco." Josh smiles broadly. "I have my memory back, guys."

Quick as a superhero, I rescue the dishes as Tony and Stephen rush to hug him.

"This is so much fun." Josh turns to me. "Honey, can we do the same for all our guests when they arrive?"

Before I can answer, Martha says, "That's a great idea. I can't wait to see the look on Chad and Franki's faces."

"And what about Jaris and Maddox, not to mention Dr. Hakala?" Sarah slaps her hands together. "That will be priceless."

Martha looks at Tony and Stephen. "This is what you have to do." She frowns. "Sad faces when the doorbell ring."

"Like this?" Tony asks, curling his lips down.

"A little over the top, sweetheart." Stephen points to his face. "More like this, right Martha?"

"You've got it."

The doorbell rings.

"Places, everyone," Sarah orders. "And don't let me see a single smile."

Josh salutes her.

He's right. This is fun. "Ready?" I ask the sad sacs.

They nod, looking absolutely downcast.

Smiling, I look out the peephole. "It's Chad and Franki with their spouses. And more food, guys."

The second I open the door, Franki sees Josh and runs to him. "Oh, Josh. What's wrong?"

"Surprise. Nothing's wrong. Your birthday is two days after mine. You hate your middle name, but I think June is a lovely name. You and Candi are married. Chad and I were your best men. And—"

"Oh, my God, you got your memory back." She hugs him as Chad rushes over.

"I'm so happy," Chad says. "Can you still sing and play the guitar?"

He grins. "Let's just see. What do you say?"

"Let's do it."

Chad picks up a bass and Franki goes to the keyboard.

Josh straps on a guitar and steps up to a microphone. "One. Two. Three. Four."

He starts singing and Chad and Franki join in.

The new arrivals are stunned when they see Josh singing and playing.

I do my best to clue everyone in. S & M help get the food set up in the kitchen. Tony and Stephen make sure everyone has something to drink.

An hour later, our apartment is filled to the max. I can't believe this many people can fit. There has to be over a hundred friends welcoming Josh back home. Actually, they don't fit. Even our patio is standing room only, and there are more out in the courtyard.

All our neighbors are here, even the ones from the new complex, Cardinal Gardens, because Grammy invited them. She, Pappy, and

Jenny have decided to move to Dallas. S & M and Oliver are thrilled since Josh's grandparents have agreed to manage the complex for them. Jenny is transferring to the local university. Josh couldn't be happier.

Mom brings me a plate of food. "Even the host should eat, sweetheart."

"Thanks. Where's your boyfriend?"

"He's helping Tony and Stephen man the bar."

"You're really getting serious, aren't you?"

She grins shyly. "You might say that."

"I like him, and so does Tony. We just want you to be happy."

"I am happy, Nicco."

Looking like the perfect example of health, Grayson steps over to me as Red Shimmer starts their second set. "Hello, Mrs. Mantonvani."

"Hi, Marshal."

He turns to me. "Great party."

"We have a lot to celebrate, Grayson. He looks happy, doesn't he?"

"Yes, he does," he says in a fatherly tone. "I'm happy too. This day has been a long time coming for Josh. Actually, for both of you."

"Yes, it has."

"By the way, I spoke with the Dallas County DA's office. They want to talk to you and your brother Tony about that murder ten years ago. They're putting together a case against Jaz and Digs and want you both to testify."

"I'd be happy to."

Mom grabs my hand and looks at Grayson. "I tried to set the record straight years ago, but no one would listen to me back then. I would like to testify, too, if the DA needs me."

"They might need you," he says. "I'll let them know."

She squeezes my hand. "I love you, son."

"Love you, too, Mom."

She walks away.

"I'm glad this nightmare is finally over for you, Mantonvani. I'm not sure how you're able to have such a good attitude after serving ten years in prison for a crime you didn't commit. You're quite an inspiration."

"I'm no Nelson Mandela. He served twenty-seven years. I memorized many things he said when I was in prison. My favorite was this: 'For to be free is not merely to cast off one's chains, but to live in a way that respects and enhances the freedom of others.' And look around you. My life is incredible. I have so many friends, a wonderful family, and the love of my life. I couldn't be happier."

Miller and Davis walk over to us.

Davis shakes my hand and turns to Grayson. "Did you ask him yet, boss?"

"Ask me what?"

"No, I haven't, but this is as good a time as any." He looks at me. "Nicco, you impressed all three of us how you handled yourself at the warehouse. You were perfect, and you had no training."

"What are getting at, Grayson?"

"Would you ever consider getting into law enforcement? I want you on my team."

"That's quite an honor, sir, but I really want to be a pilot."

"That's perfect then," Miller says. "The US Marshal's service needs aviation enforcement officers."

"Really?"

"Oh, yeah. Besides transportation of prisoners, they have a lot of important duties."

"Just think about it," Grayson says. "Whatever you decide, I'm here to help."

"We all are," Davis adds.

"Thanks, guys. I appreciate this more than you know. I will think about it."

When the band takes a break, I bring a bottle of water to Josh. "You guys sound amazing."

"Next set, I want you to join us on the keyboards, honey." He takes a sip of water. "I want to show you off."

"Sure. I'd love to."

Jenny walks up with Dr. Hakala, Jaris, and Maddox in tow.

"They insisted on checking on you, Lee. I mean Josh. Which do you prefer?"

"I don't care, sweetheart." He looks at his doctors. "I'm fine, as you can see."

"Let the doctors be the judge of that." She turns to the medical trio.

Maddox winks at Josh. "Let me take your pulse."

Josh extends his arm.

"Mm. Good." Maddox looks at Jaris. "Sixty beats. Perfect."

"Excellent." Jaris places his hand on Josh's forehead. "No temperature. Dr. Hakala?"

She grins. "Stick out your tongue for me, Josh, and say 'Ah.' No germs. In my expert opinion, you're fine, but I still would like to see you in my office next week."

"Sure thing, Doc." Josh smiles. "See Jenny. Three out of three doctors say I'm healthy as a horse."

"Now, I feel better," she says in a stoic tone. "Thank you."

As she walks to Grammy and Pappy, Josh takes the mike. "May I have your attention, please?"

Everyone turns his direction.

Expecting that Josh is about to announce the band's next song, I walk back to Grayson.

But instead I hear…

"I'm sure many of you are wondering how I got my memory back. Well, I like to call it 'How I Got My Memory Back at the Great Pancake Castastrophe in Unit G.'"

I grin, seeing the confused faces around the room.

Josh continues, "If I may direct your attention to the television for a moment, with the help of my good friend Chad, who is quite technical, you'll see a photo that will explain more."

On the flat screen the image appears of our kitchen floor covered with broken dishes, half-eaten pancakes, puddles of syrup, and orange juice.

"Believe it or not, this picture was taken this morning. Nicco did a wonderful job of cleaning the mess up. Let's give him a big hand."

Everyone claps and I shake my head.

"After enjoying a delicious breakfast that Nicco had made for us, I was on my way upstairs to take a shower, anxious to...uh...well...I asked Nicco to join me."

Laughter breaks out.

Josh winks at me. "Don't laugh. We're saving money on our water bill."

More laughter.

"Anyway, I heard a horrible crash in the kitchen."

"I bet it was because Nicco was anxious to join you in the shower," someone shouts out.

The crowd erupts in hysterics.

"Hush, everyone," Martha says with a smile. "Let Josh finish. I want to know everything."

"Thank you, Martha. I believe that most of you know that I was in the witness protection program for several years. I had witnessed a horrific murder in Chicago and had testified against the killer."

I hear several people's exclamation of shock at that news.

"If you haven't heard the story, that man standing next to Nicco is Marshal Grayson. He can tell you all about it."

Grayson grins and whispers to me. "I'm going to make him pay for that one."

"Anyway, when I heard the crash, in my mind I was literally back to that terrible day in 2010. It felt so real. My heart was racing. But the moment was different. I saw Nicco in the place of the victim, about to be shot. Still immersed in the nightmare, I ran back to the kitchen and tackled Nicco to the floor, believing I was protecting him from the killer. When Nicco yelled my name, it snapped me back to the present, with my memory completely in tact. I remembered everything." He motions to his family. "My sweet sister Jenny and my wonderful grandparents. My two bandmates. All my wonderful neighbors. Grayson and his men, who have been protecting me all these years. I remembered this apartment. My car. All the places I've lived and names I've had. All of it came back when Nicco dropped those dishes." Josh looks at me. "Come up here."

I step next to him and he puts his arms around me.

"But most of all, I remembered how much in love I am with you. You and I have been through so much. We've lost so many years. I don't want to waste another day." He gets down on one knee. "I don't have a ring yet, but I do love you with all my heart. Niccolo Mantonvani, will you marry me?"

I get down on my knee. "Only if you'll marry me, too, Leroy Brown, Michael Long, Kevin Curtis, Elmer Abbott, Josh White, and whatever other name you've used."

"Yes. I'll marry you."

"And, yes, I'll marry you too." I pull him into my arms and we kiss.

The crowd cheers as Chad and Franki start to play my favorite Red Shimmer song "Forever With You Begins Today."

Chapter 33

J *osh*

THE PHONE RINGS.

Since Nicco is in the shower, I jump out of bed to answer the call.

"Josh, this is Stephen."

"Who?" I grin. "Just kidding."

He laughs. "You're awful, Josh White."

"How many Hail Marys do I need to say, Father?"

"More than you have time for." Another laugh. "I know the party ran late. I hope I didn't wake you."

"No. We woke up an hour ago, but just taking our time to ease into the day. What can I do for you?"

"Mrs. Clark's attorney called me earlier this morning. He would like for all of us who were listed in her will to meet at his office at two this afternoon. Will that work for you and Nicco?"

"Yeah. Sure. We don't have any plans. Text me the address."

"Great. See you there."

I put my phone away and walk into the bathroom.

Nicco is drying off. "Hey, sweetheart. Who was that on the phone?"

"Stephen. Apparently Mrs. Clark mentioned us in her will and her attorney wants us to meet with everyone else at his office this afternoon."

"Really? She mentioned us in her will."

"Apparently so. I wonder what she left us."

"I bet she's giving me that antique clock in her hallway. The first time I visited her home, I mentioned how much I liked the clock. She told me how she acquired it on a trip to South Africa with her late husband, which led us into a long discussion about my hero, Nelson Mandela."

"I don't have a clue what she left me, but I'm just honored that she even thought of me."

"I totally agree." He smiles. "But I do love that clock."

NICCO and I walk into Mr. Taylor's office. The receptionist leads us to a large conference room with a flat screen where our friends are already waiting.

"There are two seats next to us," Tony says, waving us over to him and Stephen.

After we sit down, Mr. Taylor, a distinguished-looking man with silver hair, walks into the room.

I immediately recognize him as a member of Stephen's church.

"Thank you all for coming on such short notice, but I knew you would be anxious to hear Mrs. Clark's last will and testament. As you know, Mrs. Clark was a take-charge woman, never leaving any loose ends. She told me, and I quote, 'That if my will is on television, no one can argue about my intentions.' So without further ado, I'm going to let her tell you the rest. Nancy, dim the lights."

As the lights go down, sweet Mrs. Clark appears on the screen. Seeing her again makes us all smile.

"Is this on, Bill?" she asks, looking off to the side.

"Yes, ma'am. Go ahead."

"Thank you." Her gaze returns forward. It's like she's looking at each of us. "Hi, everyone. If you're watching this, I'm already dead. But don't think for one minute I'm not there with you right now. Hi, Sarah. Hi, Martha."

"Julia always knew just what to say," Sarah whispers to Martha, but we can all hear her.

"There's Father Stephen and his husband Tony. And sweet Nicco and Josh. Hi, boys. And look, there's Oliver and Adam…"

As Mrs. Clark continues calling the roll, I hold Nicco's hand. When Stephen told me about the reading of her will, I thought this was going to be sad. But it isn't. It's actually joyful.

"Most of you don't know this, but I'm—or should I say *was,* especially under the circumstances of my passing—very very very rich. I didn't flaunt that fact. My late husband invested quite well. So that's why I wanted you here. So you could hear from me exactly what I want to leave each of you. First of all, my precious Father Stephen, I love you so much. You're like a grandson to me. More like a great-grandson, if I'm honest, but don't tell anyone." She giggles.

We all laugh.

"The church has doubled in attendance since you became our rector. We've outgrown the old sanctuary. Therefore, I've instructed Bill, my attorney, to purchase the land adjacent to the Episcopal Church of the Beloved Disciple, as well as leaving one million dollars for a building fund."

"I can't believe it," Stephen says.

"In addition, I happen to know that dreadful salary you're receiving and I've never heard you complain. Therefore, I'm leaving you and Tony one million dollars, and the taxes are already paid."

"One million dollars," Tony says. "Wow."

"My dear friends, Sarah and Martha, but who everyone else

likes to call S & M." Mrs. Clark starts laughing again. "I know what that means. I've read *Fifty Shades of Grey*. Sorry, Father Stephen."

"No need to be sorry, Mrs. Clark," he says. "It's a good book and I know where you are."

Once again, we all laugh.

"I know Harvey beat me to the punch and paid off the note to Mockingbird Place and helped you get that new complex Cardinal Gardens. But, you have always told me how you both would like to travel. I think one million dollars will cover that, don't you?"

"Oh, my God, Julia," S & M say in unison.

Sarah hugs Martha. "Of course it will cover the costs."

"Sarah and I never expected anything like this."

"And don't worry, ladies. The taxes are paid. And now to my favorite babies in the whole world: Oliver and Adam's sweet boys, Mac and Link; LaShaya and Hayden's precious little girl Alison Marie; and Trace, Luke, Ava and Harrison's little Mick. Moms and dads, don't you worry, I've set up a college fund for all of them."

The happy parents are stunned and thrilled.

As she continues letting everyone know what she's left him or her, my curiosity grows. What did she leave Nicco and what did she leave me? I really hope he gets that antique clock. Me? I would just like something to remember her by.

"And now, last but not least. Nicco and Josh."

We sit up straight in our chairs, like we're her students and she's our teacher.

"To Niccolo Mantonvani, I bequest you the antique clock in my hallway. I remember how much you admired it and the lovely afternoon we had talking about Nelson Mandela."

I squeeze his hand and see the wide smile that appears on his face.

"I just love that clock," he whispers to me.

"And to Joshua White, though I really doubt that's your real name…"

Everyone turns my direction.

"No. I never told her. She must have figured it out somehow."

"That's our Julia," Martha says. "I always thought she could read minds. Now I know she could."

"If you're all through discussing what I said about Josh's name, we'll continue."

"It's like she's watching us from the great beyond," Tony says.

"Josh, you liked the painting above my fireplace, right?"

I answer her aloud, "Yes, ma'am."

A few chuckles from the group remind me this is a video.

"It's yours."

Nicco puts his arm around me. "That's awesome, sweetheart. It's a beautiful painting."

"I also think you would enjoy the candelabras on each end of the mantle. But then I know you would need the sofa to go with that. And Nicco really likes those chairs. So how about I give you boys all the furniture. Wait. Where are you going to put all the furniture in that small apartment? That will never do. Mm." She snaps her fingers. "I've got it. You need the house too."

"What?" Nicco and I blurt out together.

"It's all yours, boys. And yes, the taxes have been paid. You may wonder why I gave it to both of you. I'm hoping by now you realize what I figured out a long time ago. That you are perfect together. Mm. As I look down from heaven I can see you have figured it out. Good for you."

"Now she's freaking me out," Tony says with a laugh, and we all join in.

I have no idea how she knew Nicco and I would end up together.

"To answer your questions, the older you get, the smarter and wiser you get. At least that's how it's been for me. Nicco, I can only imagine how hard it was for you those ten years in prison. Josh, I don't know your full story, but I sense you've suffered great losses too. So on top of the house and furniture, all taxes paid, I'm throwing in one million dollars."

Once again, Nicco and I are shocked.

"And I hope you're as wise as my late husband and will invest it. And when you're old and gray like me, you'll look around and find some deserving young people and pass it on like I have to you. I love you all so very much. You're like my children. Be happy."

The screen goes dark.

Nicco and I hug each other. Then we join all our friends to celebrate this wonderful woman's generosity. We are her legacy.

icco

I GET the warning text from Chad. "Listen up, everyone," I say. "That was Chad. He's just around the corner with the birthday boy. Time to find your hiding places and be quiet."

I watch as our friends jump behind furniture, into closets, and squeeze into corners. There has to be two hundred people here, but we have plenty of room. I still can't believe I live here with Josh. This is our home.

Thank you, Mrs. Clark.

Because of her, I'm now part owner of McBain-Mantonvani Charters and Flight School. Having my pilot's license is a dream come true for me. It will take a little longer to get my commercial license, but I have all the time in the world.

I turned down Grayson's offer. Too much travel. But I did agree to consult with him and help with any cases he, Miller and Davis have in Dallas that I can.

I peek out the front window and see Red Shimmer's new van, which Chad bought with the money Mrs. Clark left him, pull up into our driveway.

"It's him." I slide next to Officer Mike, who we became friends with the past few weeks. He moved into our old apartment at Mockingbird Place. He has fit right in.

The door opens and we all yell, "Surprise!"

Josh smiles. "Are you trying to pay me back for my surprise last month?"

S & M walk in with the cake, candles burning, and we all sing the birthday song, with Chad and Franki accompanying us on their guitars.

I put my arms around Josh. "Did we get you?"

"Oh, yeah, you got me." He kisses me. "You got me good, honey. You got me forever."

About the Author

Lee Swift, who writes under several pen names including Kris Cook, creates novels, short stories, screenplays and more.

With an unquenchable thirst to experience all his life journey has to offer, Lee and hubby love travel but still call Dallas, Texas home.

Join [HERE] to get updates on Lee.

Also by Lee Swift

Novels

Morvicti Blood *(Supernatural Thriller)*

Cupid's Arrow *(Gay Fantasy Romance)*

Three to Play *(Menage MMF Romance)*

(All series listed in best reading order)

Mockingbird Place

(Gay Romance Series)

The Marine in Unit A

The Cowboy in Unit E

The Fireman in Unit C

The Doctor in Unit H

The Fighter in Unit J

Holiday Beaus (Novella)

The Musician in Unit G

The Cop in Unit B

Wolf Pack

(Menage MFM Romance Trilogy)

Secret Cravings

Primal Desires

Delicious Hunger

Eternal Trio Series

(Gay Menage Fantasy Romance)

Levi's Rogues

Perfection

Writing with Lana Lynn
(Thrillers)

Lexi's Protector *(Men Without A Cause)*

Liz's Guardian *(Men Without A Cause)*

Secret Diary Series as Kris Cook
(Erotic Straight BDSM Trilogy)

Mia's Spanking Diary

Misty's Bondage Diary

Lea's Ménage Diary